Blood Bred Series, Book 2: From the Heart

By JennaKay Francis

Writers Exchange E-Publishing
http://www.writers-exchange.com

Dedication

Thanks to Jaeger for introducing me to Baris. And to Liz for helping me understand him.

From The Heart

Baris looked back at Anika, then without another word, he pulled her up, embracing her tightly. She gasped in surprise and tried to wrest away. For the first time in their relationship, Baris allowed his Vector magic to surface. He stared deep into her eyes, seducing her with his power. Her struggles ceased as she was swept into his hypnotic spell.

Baris quickly pushed her dark hair aside and bit into her neck. She let out a little cry but did not try to stop him. He fed ravenously, not having done so for over a week. As usual, his body began to react to her closeness, her scent, her taste. One hand tangled in her hair, while the other slid along her back.

Anika pressed against him, her breathing quick and shallow. Her hands caught at his shirt, pulled him closer. For a moment, it looked as if she might also succumb to her desires. Then, with a violent shudder, she fought her way clear of him. Pain and anger clouded her features.

"Go away!" she screamed, tears again flooding her eyes--

Baris lowered himself to the boulder in the meadow. He stared out over the vast expanse of grass and flowers, taking in the riot of colors that tumbled down the slopes toward the river. Sunlight caught the wild rapids, sparkling like golden flames. It was a scene he had longed to be a part of, had been until now. Now, everything he loved, everything he held dear, was threatened by something he could not explain and didn't want to accept.

A cool breeze played over his cheeks and hands, and his dark gaze wandered to the small village nestled near the river's edge. Smoke curled from several chimneys, lazing into the morning air. Sheep and goats grazed nearby, tended by several sleepy clan members. Most of the village children were still asleep, snug in their beds, safe and secure under their parents' watchful eyes. But not his son. If Baris knew Thale, the boy was already up and investigating his world as only a two-year-old could. Thale, with Anika's blue eyes and pale complexion and his father's penchant for introspective moodiness. Mere thoughts of the energetic toddler broadened Baris' smile and, at the same time, drove pain deep into his soul.

With a wistful sigh, he rose. He was an imposing figure, lithe, well over six feet tall, with the pale skin, dark eyes and raven-black hair of the true Vector. His appearance set him apart, so it was rare for a Vector to be able to retain a true appearance in public. Instead, they usually shapeshifted to something a little more humanlike.

Yet, this was one of the reasons Baris felt so comfortable in this village. Here, he was allowed to be himself, to appear as he wanted, without repercussions. And, more importantly, here he was allowed to satisfy his requirement for human blood without having to either seduce victims or hunt them down. And he owed it to Jaeger and his wife, Rhiannon.

Four years earlier, Rhiannon, and by extension her entire clan, and the Vectors had established a relationship. The clan were Bleeders; their bodies produced abnormally high levels of iron that could prove fatal if it were not bled off. But they were also witches, which proved a hazardous combination. Use of their magic only increased the already high content of iron in their blood, making the need to be bled even stronger. Many witches had died trying to bleed themselves. A partnership with the Vectors had been sought in desperation. Vectors needed blood. Bleeders had the blood to give. It was an equitable situation for both parties.

However, falling in love with Anika had been a delightful bonus. Baris had never expected more than a business relationship. In fact, he had never expected to find love in the true meaning of the word at all.

Like most Vectors, Baris was a product of careful planning. His father had been the Vector Sovereign; his mother had done nothing more than donate her egg. The embryo they created was given into the care of a

Chosen, one of a special kind of Vector that carried, then implanted fertile embryos in human women. The one who carried, then bore, Baris had not survived long after his birth. Her sacrificial blood belonged to the Chosen who had impregnated her. And to the child she had carried.

As a child, Baris was raised in the Vector's Lair, a vast underground system of caverns nestled deep within a towering mountain range. He had many guardians and teachers but no true parents. It was the Vector way and Baris had accepted it. At least, he had until he had finally ventured from the Lair. It was then that he had seen the way humans related, how they paired and mated. Eventually, he had witnessed the deep love and commitment between Rhiannon and Jaeger, her husband. He couldn't explain the yearning that witnessing such love and devotion between two people had created in him. It was something he decided he wanted for himself.

Yet, he had never allowed himself to expect that it could happen to him. It was a part of his heart that he had shut off. Until Anika.

In fact, she had first approached him. He had tried to be professional, businesslike, although he was at once taken with her beauty. Her eyes in particular. While his were the almost black of a pure Vector, hers were the most incredible blue he had ever seen. They reminded him of the summer sky, something he had come to love after so many years in the Lair. And she was like a breath of summer herself, a new life that beckoned to him, called to him. Still, he held her away, sure that her interest in him was only one of business. He told himself repeatedly that she could never have any other interest in him. Then she began coming about more frequently, sought him out over other Vectors when she needed to be bled, and slowly chipped away at his resolve. It was a monumental, and frightening, day for Baris when he realized that he indeed loved her. He was terrified that his love would not be returned. But Anika had assuaged that worry with one, long, lingering, passionate kiss. A kiss Baris had returned with his heart.

The last four years had been filled with happiness and contentment such that he had never experienced before. Now--

A movement caught his eye and he turned toward the young, brown-haired woman climbing the slopes toward him. He moved to meet her as she reached him with a smile.

"You wanted to see me?" she asked, dark eyes glowing.

Baris studied her for a moment before nodding. He had known her for only a short time. She had returned to the village six months earlier after living for many years in a neighboring city. She had been a great support to him in the last several months while his life fell apart around him, and although the words were painful to say, Baris felt she should know what he had planned.

"Yes, Deirdre. I wanted to say goodbye."

"Goodbye?" She looked up at him in surprise. "You're leaving? Why?"

"Anika has asked me to leave," he said quietly. The words drove daggers of hurt through his heart.

A small gasp escaped the woman and she laid one hand on his arm. "Oh, Baris, I'm so sorry. Did she say why?"

"No. I questioned her but she didn't seem to have any reason." He paused, trying to quiet the tremor in his voice. "She just demanded that I leave. Now. I am abiding by her wishes."

"But where will you go?"

"I have thought hard about that. I am going to seek out Vail. He may have an answer to this change in behavior. I must know what I have done to cause this."

"Perhaps it was not you at all, Baris," Deirdre said. "You have been nothing but kind and gentle with Anika. I would place the blame on her and her alone."

Baris looked down at the slight woman before him. Dark curls fell in tangles well past her shoulders, framing a face the color of moonlight. Her brown eyes were almond-shaped, ringed with long dark lashes that brushed her cheeks when she looked down. She was emotional, warm, caring and genuinely concerned about him. Perhaps more so then she should have been. She was beautiful in every way but she did nothing for his heart. That belonged to Anika. He had to find out what had caused her change in affection and Vail might have the answer. The problem was finding him.

Baris clearly remembered his last visit with Anika's young cousin. It had been on this very spot, where just six months ago he had felt firsthand Vail's own pain at a failed relationship.

"So, you're leaving?"

Vail shrugged. "What point is there in staying? It's clear that Rachael isn't interested."

"I'm sorry that things didn't work out."

Again, Vail shrugged. "That's life, Baris. I could use the Vector 'charm' Jaeger gave me, but, like he once said, I would rather that she come to me on her own."

Baris smiled. He remembered how Jaeger had given Vail some of his own blood to save the young man's life. And he remembered Jaeger's anguish over what it would mean to Vail. "You're a wise man, Vail." He lifted his head as another young man arrived in the meadow. "Ah, Baul. You are accompanying Vail on his travels then?"

The young Vector nodded. "We can keep each other company. And keep each other healthy as well."

Baris laughed and clapped Baul on the shoulder then shot a sidelong glance at Vail. "Are you sure you're all right with this?"

Vail blushed. "I am. I realize that I will still need to be bled and Baul here is very good at doing so. Besides, he's great company. And we have a lot in common."

"Oh?" Baris looked at the two young men in turn. One was a Vector, one a human. One six feet tall, the other barely over five. "How so?"

They grinned together. "We both like women!" they answered in unison.

Baris laughed again. "I see. And that's what you'll be searching for on this great journey?"

"Of course," Vail replied. "What better?"

"What better, indeed," Baris answered. "Well, take with you my blessings and good wishes for a happy outcome."

"Thank you," Vail said. "Time to do that shapeshifting bit, Baul. I don't intend to walk."

"Oh, perfect," Baul grumbled. "You have just enough Vector blood in you to seduce the women, but not enough to share the rigors of the journey."

Vail grinned. "Blame Jaeger for that. He's the one who gave me the blood in the first place."

Baul scowled teasingly at Vail and shapeshifted to a horse. Vail groaned.

"A horse! I was hoping for a dragon or something like that. I'll be too sore to seduce anyone if I have to ride half the country on horseback."

Baul snorted and tossed his head.

Baris chuckled. "I think you'd better be happy he's doing this much," he told Vail. "Keep complaining and you'll be walking."

Vail grimaced. "Fine, fine. This will do."

"You take good care of yourselves," Baris said. "And be careful. There are those who do not take kindly to Vectors. Or witches."

Vail nodded, swung astride the horse and they rode off.

Now, Baris wished Vail hadn't gone at all. He didn't feel comfortable talking to other members of the clan about his floundering relationship with Anika. Except for Deirdre. For some reason, she brought out the words, the emotions, the pain he was harboring. She had become a safe haven for him lately, although he had not really gone looking. He still couldn't fathom why he seemed so loose-lipped with her. It was as if he had known her all of his life. And yet, they had met only six months ago.

"What do you think Vail could do?" Deirdre asked him, interrupting his moody thoughts.

Baris shook his head. "I don't know. But I'm not willing to simply walk away from Anika, or my son. I need to know what has happened to her...to us."

Deirdre tightened her grip on his arm, her gaze wistful pleading. "I could come with you."

He started. "Why? Your family is here, Deirdre. You just returned to them. Why would you leave them so soon?"

"My family? They wouldn't stand in my way. I know that much. Besides, you're going to need a--helper. I can do that. Please, Baris, let me come along."

Baris considered. What she said was true. As a Vector, he needed blood daily. Still, since his marriage to Anika, he had tasted no other but her. He didn't know if he could. Feeding was linked to a sexual response in him at his age. He had only come into his Growth three years ago and he still hadn't adjusted completely. There were very few times that he didn't become sexually aroused when he fed. Thankfully, Anika didn't seem to mind in the slightest. Baris was not willing to risk a sexual arousal with Deirdre even though he knew it would be a purely physical reaction.

He shook his head. "It might be too dangerous, Deirdre. You'd be better off staying here."

"I have nothing here, Baris. I would love to see the world but I probably never will just because I'm a woman. I feel so tied down here."

Baris couldn't help but smile. "From what Anika told me, you've spent the last ten years exploring the world."

Deirdre pouted. "Not really. I was but a child when I was sent to the city. I wasn't allowed to do much of anything except attend my schooling. But, Baris, I want to see new things, go new places, meet different and exciting people. I'll never get the chance to do that the way things are going. If you're going to travel, I would like to join you. We could help each other along the way. Please, at least say you'll consider it. Please?"

Baris hesitated. He knew what it was like to feel trapped, imprisoned by what you were. He was a Vector, trapped by rumors and frightful tales of what he was capable of. She was no less trapped inside a body that assumed a particular lifestyle for her. Yes, Baris could well empathize with her need to escape her shackles.

Taking his silence as consent, Deirdre rushed on. "When were you planning to leave?"

"As soon as I can get a direction. I need to have someone scry for Vail."

"I can do that!" Deirdre cried. She tugged on his arm. "Come to the river with me. I can do it right now."

Baris glanced at the village, at his house. He could see smoke coming from the chimney now. Anika was up, preparing breakfast for Thale. He should be there as well, helping her. But she didn't want his help. She had made that quite clear the previous night. He sighed and nodded.

They walked down the gentle slope to a spot on the river that ran calmer than the rest. Baris settled down in the grass at the water's edge while Deirdre prepared to cast her spell. It didn't take her long, though Baris saw no image in the water at the angle he sat from her. He moved forward to get a better look, but the image had disappeared. Deirdre looked at him with a smile.

"He's to the north of us, near the mountains," she said. "There is a sizeable village there." She giggled. "It looked like he and Baul were having a good time together. They were surrounded by women."

Baris smiled, wondering if the young men were using their Vector magic to charm. He rose, brushing the dirt and grass from his breeches. "Then, it looks as if I go north."

Deirdre looked up at him. Baris drew a long, slow breath, unable to resist the silent pleading he saw in her dark eyes. "All right, you may come along."

She leapt to her feet, wrapped her arms about him, then stood on her tiptoes and kissed him soundly on the cheek. "Thank you, Baris, thank you so much! I'll go home and pack straight away."

"Deirdre!" He caught at her arm. "Perhaps it would be best to keep our traveling arrangements to ourselves. If others know we are traveling together, it might start gossip."

She frowned. "But it will be obvious, Baris. We'll both be leaving at the same time. Better to be honest about it."

Baris grimaced. "I suppose you're right," he murmured, though he had no idea how he would break the news to Anika. He released his hold on Deirdre. "Go then. I'll meet you here in an hour's time."

She nodded and hurried away, her excitement rushing over him like a warm gush of air. A shudder of trepidation ran through him, but he brushed it aside and descended the hill. As he neared his cottage, he slowed, wondering how he would be received this morning. Thale met him just outside door. At least the little boy was happy to see him.

"Papa!" Thale shouted in delight. He rushed toward Baris, his chubby little legs moving as fast as he could make them.

Baris caught him just as he stumbled and pitched forward. "Here now," he said gently. "You need to be careful. You'll hurt yourself." He hugged the child to him, breathing deeply of the scent of innocence.

"Where you were?" Thale demanded.

"I went for a walk. Where's Mama?"

"In." Thale pointed toward the house.

Baris again drew a deep breath, then carried the little boy into the house. It was dark and warm inside, the only light coming from the fire. The shutters were still closed, though daylight attempted to sneak past them. Baris set Thale down and opened the shutters while he sought out Anika.

She was lying on the bed in the adjoining room, her face pale and drawn. She winced and turned away from the light. "Why did you open those?" she whined.

"It's morning, Anika. Are you not feeling well again?"

"I'm fine. I'm just tired. It would have been nice if you had stayed to light the fire and get Thale's breakfast. Where were you?"

Baris went into the bedroom. "I went for a walk. I'm sorry about the fire. I thought I had put on enough wood before I left. I'll fetch more."

"Don't bother. I already got it." Anika drew the covers up around her neck as if she felt chilled, though the room was quite warm.

Baris approached her warily. He could smell iron. The scent hung like a heavy blanket over the room. Anika hadn't been bled for almost a week and she was building up toxic levels of iron in her system. Still, she had refused to let Baris help her. He full well knew the consequences if she did not rid her body of the excess iron.

"You need to be bled," he said softly.

"Leave me alone!"

He dropped down on the side of the bed and reached to touch her shoulder. She shrank away from him.

"Go away, Baris."

"Anika, you need to be bled," he said again. "If you don't want me to do it, then find someone else. But, please, for Thale's sake, it must be done. You cannot care for him if you are ill."

"I can care for him just fine!" she snapped, turning to face him.

He was struck with her pallor, the dark circles under her blue eyes. She had lost weight and her cheeks were sunken and bony. His heart broke looking at her, feeling her disgust of him.

"You're sick, Ani," he whispered. "Please, let me help you."

She was silent for a moment in which tears suddenly welled in her eyes. "Baris, I..." She broke off, wincing as if in pain. The hardness returned to her face, her tone. "I thought I asked you to leave. I want you to go, Baris. Just leave. Thale and I can manage quite well on our own." She pulled the covers up again and turned away.

Baris' heartache turned to anger. He would not let her do this. He would not let her destroy herself like this. No matter what she thought of him, she had Thale to consider. She couldn't care for him if she was so ill. Baris leaned back and peered into the front room. Thale was sprawled on the floor, teasing the cat with a bit of string.

Baris looked back at Anika, then without another word, he pulled her up, embracing her tightly. She gasped in surprise and tried to wrest away. For the first time in their relationship, Baris allowed his Vector magic to surface. He stared deep into her eyes, seducing her with his power. Her struggles ceased as she was swept into his hypnotic spell.

Baris quickly pushed her dark hair aside and bit into her neck. She let out a little cry but did not try to stop him. He fed ravenously, not having done so for over a week. As usual, his body began to react to her closeness, her scent, her taste. One hand tangled in her hair, while the other slid along her back.

Anika pressed against him, her breathing quick and shallow. Her hands caught at his shirt, pulled him closer. For a moment, it looked as if she might also succumb to her desires. Then, with a violent shudder, she fought her way clear of him. Pain and anger clouded her features.

"Go away!" she screamed, tears again flooding her eyes.

"Mama?" Thale appeared at the doorway, his small face puzzled and scared.

Baris stood and scooped the little boy into his arms. Anika shot from the bed, reaching as though to snatch Thale away from him, only to sway unsteadily.

"What are you doing? Put him down!" she demanded.

"No," Baris said quietly. "I cannot leave here without him. You need time alone, Anika. Time to recover from whatever is troubling you. I will take Thale to stay with Jaeger and Rhiannon for a few days."

"No!" She started forward again, then staggered and fell to her knees. Thale began to cry and clung to his father's neck. A sharp rap on the front door interrupted and Baris backed away from Anika, keeping one eye on her, while he answered it. Deirdre stood on the front step, a pack in her hand, excitement in her dark eyes.

"Are you ready?" she asked.

Baris frowned, annoyance picking at him. "I asked you to meet me at the river," he murmured.

"What's she doing here?" Anika demanded.

Baris drew a slow, controlled breath, his gaze shifting momentarily to his wife then back to Deirdre. "Do me a favor, Deirdre. Take Thale for a short walk. I need to talk to Anika alone."

Deirdre gave a slight grimace but she placed her pack on the stoop. Baris handed her the little boy, who whimpered and wriggled until she had to either set him down or drop him. Baris hunkered down before him.

"Go with Deirdre," he commanded gently. "I need to get your clothes packed. Uncle Jaeger and Aunt Rhiannon will be so happy to see you. And what of your cousin? You always like to play with him."

Thale pouted, his gaze moving to the inside of the house. "Mama come, too?"

Baris hesitated. "I don't know. We'll see. Go along, now." He gave the little boy a gentle shove, then stood and closed the door.

Anika had managed to get to her feet and was standing in the bedroom doorway, staring at him in obvious shock. "You're going off with Deirdre, aren't you?"

Baris shook his head. "I am not 'going off' with her. In fact..." He approached her slowly, warily, "I don't wish to go at all." He stopped before her then took her hands in his. Hers were cold and clammy, limp in his grasp. "Please, Anika, please tell me what is wrong. Let me help you."

She looked up at him, tears again shining in her eyes. "Baris, I...I don't...I just don't feel well. Something--" She trembled, averted her gaze and pulled her hands from his. "Don't take Thale away from me," she pleaded in a whisper.

The words drove into Baris' heart. "I won't," he said, his resolve strengthening. "Because you're coming as well. Perhaps Jaeger can figure out what is ailing you. If not, I'll find your cousin. And if he doesn't know, I'll take you into the Lair."

He thought she would protest, was astonished when she only nodded weakly. He seized the moment. It didn't take him but a few moments to gather blankets, dried foods, water, and anything else he thought they would need in their journey to Nowles, where Anika's cousin, Rhiannon, and her half-Vector husband, Jaeger, lived. He pushed thoughts of his promise to Deirdre aside. He would have to leave her here. He could shapeshift into a dragon large enough to hold Anika and Thale but carrying three might be more than he could handle.

He helped Anika dress in her long woolen skirt and linen blouse. He didn't bother with brushing out her hair, just gathered it up and slipped it beneath a linen bonnet, then tied her cloak about her shoulders. All the while, Anika stood, limp and lifeless, not helping, not protesting his actions, although her face was a mask of hard concentration. He took her by the shoulders and looked into her eyes.

"Baris," she murmured, leaning against him, exhausted. "Help me."

The words were unexpected but welcome. He hugged her and guided her from the house. Deirdre waited in the small patch of grass outside. Thale ran to him the moment he left the house.

"Deirdre, there's been a change of plans," he said, lifting the child. "I'm taking both Thale and Anika with me to Jaeger. Maybe he can help her."

"But what about me?"

"I can come back for you if you really desire to see the world, Deirdre. But I must take care of Ani and my son first."

Deirdre shot Anika a glance. "And how are you planning to get to Jaeger's? Anika doesn't look like she will be able to stay astride a horse for very long."

"I am not going on horseback. I am going to shapeshift to a dragon. I can carry both Anika and Thale that way."

"But how will Anika be able to hold onto Thale?" Deirdre asked. "She looks so weak. What if he escapes her grasp and falls?"

The thought hadn't occurred to Baris, but now it presented with a very real horror. He looked at his small son, then at Anika. She looked barely able to stand. There was no way she could hold onto a squirming two-year-old and keep her seat on a soaring dragon at the same time.

"If you could carry all of us," Deirdre suggested reasonably, her gaze locked on Anika's, "I could hold Thale. Maybe even help hold Anika on as well."

Anika glared at her. "No," she said stiffly. "I can hold my own son." She abruptly straightened. "As a matter of fact, I don't even want to go. And I don't want Thale to go either." She made a move as if to pull the little boy away from Baris.

He moved out of her reach. "No, Ani. We're going. It's settled. You need help. I don't know what kind but it's obvious I can't do anything for you on my own."

"I don't need help!" Anika snapped, then rubbed at her head. "Why can't everyone just leave me alone? I just want to be left alone." She turned back toward the house but Baris stopped her.

"We're going to Jaeger," he said firmly. "If he can find nothing wrong, then I will leave you in peace. I promise."

"And Thale?"

Baris looked at the little boy. "He is also *my* son, Anika."

Her face darkened with anger. "If you take him from me, Baris, I will hunt you down," she snarled. "I swear it. I will hunt you down and I will do whatever it takes to reclaim my son."

Baris stared at her, her words stinging. He shot a glance at Deirdre, then handed Thale to her before returning his attention to Anika. "I would never take Thale from you," he said, his own anger finally aroused. "I hope that you will make the same promise to me."

Anika said nothing. She was looking at Deirdre, her gaze locked with the other woman's, yet she made no move to snatch Thale away. Baris started as an angry shout went up. He turned to see a well-muscled man storming his way. He recognized the man at once...the town smithie, Holt. Holt had never been friendly with Baris, but then many of the village people weren't, despite the mutually beneficial arrangement. Baris was often shunned and when he was approached, it was done with a certain wariness. It was something Baris accepted because he wanted Anika to be with her own kind. Today, however, Holt's hostility was the last thing he needed to cope with.

Deirdre let out a small huff of annoyance. "Holt," she said tightly. "I told you, it's been decided. Go away!"

"Not until I understand exactly what is going on here!" the man snapped, reaching them. He glared at Baris. "Just what are your intentions with Deirdre?"

"My intentions?" The question caught Baris off guard. He spread his hands in confusion. "I have no 'intentions' but friendship. She asked to accompany me on a trip. I agreed. That is all."

Holt's face tightened, his anger increasing, though it was not likely that he would act. He well knew of a Vector's superhuman strength, both magically and physically.

"That's all?" he sneered. "Just a little trip? Just you and her?"

"No," Baris explained. "Anika and Thale are also coming along."

That seemed to calm Holt somewhat. "And where will you go?"

Baris hesitated. He wasn't sure where, exactly, he might be going if Jaeger could do nothing for Anika. It was likely he would seek Vail, even though he had promised Anika that he would leave her alone if the visit to Jaeger failed. He would have told her anything if it meant getting her cooperation.

Still, going into the Vector's Lair was a last resort. Humans were only welcome there in dire emergencies. And though Baris felt this was such, he doubted that the Vector Sovereign, Darius, would agree.

"We won't be gone long or far," he told Holt finally. "I will return Deirdre within the week, most likely."

"The week!" Deirdre protested. "But what can I see of the world in a week?"

"Enough to know this is where you belong," Holt pronounced.

Deirdre whirled on him. "I will belong wherever I wish to belong, Holt!

Just because my father, in his infinite wisdom, has declared that I will be your wife does not mean I will. I have a mind of my own and a will of my own. I will choose my mate myself."

The rage returned to Holt's face. "One week, Deirdre! If you are not back, I will come looking for you." He brought his gaze up to meet Baris'. "And you." He spun on his heel and stormed away.

Baris watched him go, his own emotions tangling in confusion. He didn't want to intrude on clan custom; it was not his place. But he certainly didn't approve of pre-arranged marriages, especially when there didn't seem to be any feelings between the two parties. That, however, was not the most important thing on his mind right now, and he brought his thoughts back to his own situation. He had to help Anika first and foremost. Deirdre and Holt could wait.

He quickly shapeshifted into a dragon, not altogether sure that Anika would even take her place between his massive wings. He hoped that Deirdre's holding Thale would provide the incentive. It did. As soon as Deirdre climbed onto his back with the little boy, Anika followed, although her anger was almost palpable.

With a heavy sigh, Baris took flight. He winged out over the village, trying to keep his back level, terrified at the thought of losing one of his precious cargo. The ground raced past beneath him. Fields, rivers, small lakes, all disappeared as he flew onward, toward Nowles far away to the north. It would be several days before they would reach it, even at the daily distances Baris could travel as a dragon. And with Thale along, rest periods were inevitable and important. Baris couldn't expect the little boy to remain seated an entire day.

Still, Baris kept the stops to a minimum. Finally, just as the sun was setting over the distant horizon, he touched down lightly on a craggy mountain slope, thankful to find a flat place of relative size on which to land. He was exhausted, more so than he felt he should have been. He frowned, puzzled, but had little time to analyze the feeling.

Anika dismounted immediately and sank down against a large, rough-hewn boulder, holding one hand to her stomach, obviously nauseated from the long ride. Deirdre climbed down more slowly, her arms tight about a now-sleeping Thale. Baris shifted back to his Vector form and managed a small smile at his son. He had never even dreamed that the boy would be able to sleep during the flight. Or that he would so easily accept the fact that his father had turned into a huge dragon right before his eyes.

Baris scanned their immediate surroundings. They were fairly high on a gentle mountain slope. Rock tumbles were everywhere and scrub made up a goodly portion of the vegetation, but there was also a thick forest to the west and again to the east. Baris looked up the slope toward the mountain summit. He remembered that Jaeger had mentioned a pass through the mountain range. It should be somewhere close, and Baris was sure he would find it once airborne again.

He turned toward Deirdre as she placed Thale on a blanket she had pulled from one of the packs. Another small smile creased Baris' lips at the sight of his small son, sleeping so soundly even in such a desolate place as this. Another sound brought Baris around with a gasp. Anika was hunched over, retching into the brush.

"Ani!" He hurried to her side.

"Leave me be," Anika mumbled, attempting to push him away.

"No." He turned to Deirdre. "Fetch me the waterskin."

The woman complied, though she seemed uncomfortable dealing with whatever plagued Anika. Baris couldn't fault her for it...many people were uncomfortable dealing with illness. Still, he wished she could have been more empathetic. He tipped out a handful of the water and gently wiped Anika's face with it. She leaned back against the rock, her gaze moving to

Deirdre.

"You'd be better off with her," she murmured. "She's healthy and whole. And she seems to care for you. And you, for her."

Baris frowned, puzzled. He had made no overt gesture of anything more than friendship toward Deirdre. What could Anika be reading into the situation? Then Holt's question about his "intentions" came back to haunt him. He wondered if his impromptu, albeit frequent, meetings with Deirdre had suggested a meaning he hadn't intended. After all, he hadn't really planned any of those meetings but the last. And that one was only to say goodbye. Deirdre had always just seemed to show up, to be there when he was feeling alone and confused and needed to talk. She had easily filled a void in his life just at the moment he had needed it. And perhaps he had leaned a little too heavily on that support.

Baris had little real knowledge of the relationship between men and women. All that he had observed while in the Lair had been no more than friendly talk. Vector men seldom got romantically involved with either Vector or human women. The former were far too reticent to commit to what would be basically a union for eternity and humans were most often viewed as only a temporary dalliance.

In fact, if he were to be honest with himself, Baris still wasn't sure how he viewed what he had with Anika. Perhaps that was the core of their problems. He would outlive her, most likely even outlive his own son. Had he mistaken temporary lust for love, and had she seen through his self-delusion before he did? If so, he wasn't being fair to her. Still, there was something about his feelings for her, something that transcended anything he had ever experienced.

He tenderly brushed stray locks of hair from her fevered face. "Deirdre is a friend, nothing more, Ani. You are my wife, you are the one I love."

She looked up at him, her gaze wistful. "Do you, Baris? Do you really?"

The question further puzzled him. "Have I given you any reason to doubt my love?"

Anika averted her gaze without answering. Baris sighed and straightened. He recapped the waterskin and turned to Deirdre. "After I rest, we can continue. I'm afraid that I have not used my Vector magic in quite some time. I find it quite exhausting now." He turned his attention to Thale, who had wakened and was happily investigating a small hole in the rocks. At least the boy he could understand. The child's emotions were open and honest. Everything he felt, he showed. Baris approached him.

"What are you looking at?"

"Snake," Thale answered enthusiastically.

Alarm rushed through Baris and he quickly pulled the child aside. "Be careful, son. Sometimes snakes bite."

Thale frowned and examined his fingers. "No bite," he announced.

Baris smiled. "Good. I'm glad to hear that. Are you hungry?"

"Go fly more," Thale answered, gesturing at the sky.

"No, all done flying for now," Baris said with a chuckle. "Maybe more flying later. Come, sit by Mama for a while."

"No." Thale's answer was quick and firm.

Baris eyed his son in confusion. "No? Why not?"

"Not Mama," Thale replied. "Mama gone."

"What? No, Thale, that's Mama. She just isn't feeling very well right now. Come, maybe you can make her feel better."

"No! Not Mama!" Thale repeated, planting his chubby legs.

"Maybe he just means she isn't acting like normal," Deirdre put in softly. "Children notice these things."

Thale glared up at her. "You go away. Go now. Me no like you! You bad!"

"Thale!" Baris admonished. "That's not nice. I'm sorry, Deirdre. Anika's illness must be affecting him, too."

Deirdre shrugged, though her gaze was on the child. "How long will you need to rest, Baris? And just what do you hope that Jaeger will do for Anika?"

"I don't know," Baris admitted with a sigh. "It's possible that Jaeger will know what ails Anika the moment he sees her. He knows far more of humans than I do. He knows of their frailties and illnesses. And Rhiannon is a gifted healer. There couldn't be a better place to take Anika. At least, as a place to begin. If that's the case, I may not have to go after Vail at all. I would hate to disturb him on his great quest for love." He had meant the words to be light but Deirdre frowned.

"What exactly are you expecting him to solve?" she asked again.

"I don't know. Not really. It's just that whatever has happened to Anika seemed to happen so fast. I guess I'm hoping it's something simple." Baris studied her a moment. "You're a witch, Deirdre. Can you tell if there is something physically wrong with Anika?"

"No," Deirdre replied. "I'm not that skilled. Rhiannon far out-distances me when it comes to healing and such. I'm sorry."

Baris waved the apology aside, glancing at Anika, who had drifted into restless sleep. He hoped it was something as simple as an illness. That could be fixed. It might take some time and some talent, but it could be fixed. If it was just that she had lost her feelings for him, or perhaps had read through his own uncertainties--he didn't know if he could accept that.

He looked again at his son, only to find that Thale had once more stuck his hand into the dark hole in the rocks. His cry of warning mixed with Thale's shriek of pain. Baris darted forward and yanked the little boy away. Blood dripped from two small bites on his tiny finger. Thale's howls echoed on the rocky slope.

Anika came awake with a startled gasp. She struggled to her feet. "What happened?" she cried, staggering over.

"He's been bitten," Baris replied. "A snake."

"Oh, by the saints!" Anika grabbed the little boy's hand and began to squeeze the blood through the wound, at the same time murmuring magical words of healing. Thale screamed and tried to pull free. Baris held him tightly, trying to soothe him with soft words. Thale battled him furiously, finally succeeding in wresting his pudgy little hand away from Anika.

"No!" she cried. "Thale, sweetling, stop!"

"Let me help," Deirdre said. She reached out and snagged the little boy's arms.

Almost at once, he calmed, staring at her.

"Stop!" Anika hissed. "Not your magic, Deirdre. Not on my son!" She grabbed for Thale's arm to pull him away from the other woman and their eyes met.

"Ani, stop!" Baris cried, confusion raging through him. "She's only trying to help. Please, one of you just heal his finger."

Anika shuddered and pulled away. She backed up, her gaze locked on Deirdre. Then, abruptly, she whirled and bolted, disappearing in the rocky terrain. Baris' cry of alarm and disbelief followed her. Thale suddenly howled in agony, and Baris spun back to his son. The little boy tried to shake away the searing pain as the venom from the snake entered his bloodstream. Baris grabbed Thale's arm, stopping his flailing, knowing the more Thale moved, the quicker the poison would course through his body. Baris looked desperately at Deirdre.

"Can you do anything?"

She shook her head. "I told you, I don't have much in the way of magic. I was only trying to calm him so Anika could work."

Thale suddenly stopped screaming and the color drained from his face. A light sheen of sweat broke out on his brow, and he went limp. Baris stared at him in terror. Without another moment's hesitation, he bit into his own wrist, drawing blood. He seized Thale's finger, forced it to bleed once again, then let his own blood drip into the small wounds.

"What are you doing?" Deirdre whispered, her eyes wide with alarm.

"Healing him. I hope." Baris forced calm into his voice. A calm he didn't feel. He hadn't wanted to give the boy his blood, was worried about the possible outcome. Already Thale was a part of him, carried his heritage. Baris didn't know what would happen now that he also carried his blood. It could push him toward a life neither Anika nor Baris wanted for him. A life that would involve Vector magic, possibly even the need for blood. Baris grimaced, but could think of nothing else to do.

Anger exploded inside him. Why had Anika deserted her own son when he needed her most? How could she abandon the child she claimed to love so much? Baris had no answers. He looked at Thale's pale face, his half-shut eyelids with the whites showing, and gently stroked the little boy's cheek, then lay the limp form back on the blanket.

"Will he be all right now?" Deirdre asked.

"I don't know. I think so. Keep him warm. Give him water if you can get him to drink it. I need to find Anika. She can't have gotten far. I won't be gone long." He stepped back, ready to shift into an owl to allow him to better see countryside in the dark.

Thale whimpered and stirred. "Papa," he murmured.

The plea was so heartbreaking Baris paused. His gaze traveled over the rocks.

"Baris," Deirdre suggested softly, "perhaps your place is here, with Thale. He needs you. Anika has made her own choice. And did she not wish that you would leave her alone?"

Baris looked at her in surprise. "Yes, she did, but..."

"Then," Deirdre interrupted, "I think you need to respect her wishes.

She'll be back. She just needs a little time alone." She gestured at the crying child. "Be with the one who wants you now. Your son."

Baris took Thale in his arms. The little boy clung to him weakly, trembling and burying his small face against his father's neck. Baris hoped he had been swift enough in his decision to give the child some of his Vector blood. He couldn't bear the thought of losing Thale.

"I have to get him to a healer," he decided. "I have to make sure he's all right."

She nodded. "But where?"

"I must go into the Lair."

"Have you recovered enough to do that?"

"Yes. I think I can get both Thale and I there. But..."

Deirdre placed one hand on his arm. "Don't worry over me, Baris. The child comes first. Do what you must. Just promise that you'll come back for me. I don't really want to be left out here alone for too long."

"You won't be alone. As you said, Anika will come back shortly. It's getting dark and cold. And I will return as soon as I can."

Deirdre nodded, then stood on tiptoe to kiss his cheek. "Godspeed, Baris. Help Thale. I'll be here, waiting."

Baris studied her a moment longer, wondering at her understanding and compassion when even Thale's own mother had shown so little. Then, holding Thale tightly against his chest, he cast his magic and entered the Vector's Lair.

"Will he be all right?" Baris asked. His voice seemed to echo in the large underground cavern. Despite the presence of thick hangings covering the stone walls, and a fire roaring in the massive hearth, the room felt cold and clammy. He could not envision how his small son could recover in such surroundings, yet he would not complain. That Darius, Sovereign of the Vectors, had taken Thale into his own home was astounding to Baris. He knew that the little boy could not be in better hands than the most gifted of the Lair's Vectors.

Now, Darius nodded as he looked down at the pale child lying on the bed. "He will recover. The poison did manage to get into his system, despite what you and Anika did. By the way, where is Anika?"

"I--didn't think I should bring her inside," Baris said. "She is waiting for me. In fact, I need to get back. Thale, he..."

"He needs to stay put for a while," Darius interrupted. He cast Baris a questioning glance but did not quiz him further. "He'll be fine here. I'll watch over him as if he were my own."

Baris drew a deep breath and turned away, once more looking at his son. He seemed so small and frail, lying in the large bed. His skin was the color of the linen sheets surrounding him, his breathing shallow and slow. Baris bent and kissed the small forehead, wincing at the fever consuming the boy.

"I love you, Thale," he whispered. "Be strong for Papa." He straightened. "I need to get back outside," he told Darius "I will return as soon as I can. And thank you, Elder. Thank you very much." Aware of Darius's puzzled countenance, Baris cast his own magic to return to the rocky slopes where he had left Deirdre.

Night had long since descended, casting the area into darkness. Deirdre was waiting for him. Anika was not. He scanned the immediate surroundings as Deirdre got up from the small campfire she had kindled.

"She didn't return," Deirdre told him gently. "I even called for her. She didn't answer. I'm sorry."

Baris could find no words. His heart beat painfully, his breath caught in his throat. "She could be hurt," he murmured. "You saw how weak she was. I have to find her."

"Can you shift again so soon?"

The truth was, he was exhausted but he had to try. He couldn't forsake his wife, no matter her words or her actions. He nodded in answer to Deirdre's question.

"Yes, I should be able to. Please, Deirdre, forgive me for leaving you once again. I must find her." He stepped back and quickly shapeshifted into an owl.

Deirdre said nothing as he took flight. His keen eyesight raked over the dark rocks, noticing even the slightest movement, yet nowhere did he see Anika. Still, he circled, widening his search with each pass, peering into the thick forest that lay on the rocky mountains like a green-and-brown skirt. How could she have gotten so far away? Or was she hiding from him? But why? Why would she first abandon her injured child, then hide from her own husband? It didn't make any sense. Yet, Baris had to remind himself that Anika was violently ill. Who knew what she might do?

He continued his search as the night skies grew lighter, announcing the arrival of morning. Still there was no sign of Anika. Baris' despair and anger gnawed at his gut, drove him on in desperation. Just as the sun sliced the horizon, a movement caught his eye. He banked toward it.

As he drew closer, he realized what he had seen was nothing more than a large snake, slithering from its cold burrow to lie in the sun. Rage plucked at him, fueled by his fatigue and his heartache. He dove toward the snake, his great wings cupped to slow his descent. He plucked the venomous creature from the dirt with his talons, lifting it high into the air. The snake writhed and twisted in his grasp, seeking to strike. In a fury, Baris let it fall against the rocks. It hit hard, convulsed, then fell in a tangled pile to the ground below, where it lay twitching.

He was about to dive down, finish the animal off, but the fatigue he had been fighting off by sheer force of will finally overtook him. Terrified that he would lose his shift, he swiftly turned and winged back to the encampment. He landed and shapeshifted almost at the same moment, stumbling wearily.

Deirdre was on her feet at once, as if she had known he was coming back. She caught him and supported him so that he sank gently to the ground.

"You didn't find her?"

Baris shook his head, tears of frustration welling in his eyes. "I can't see how she could have gotten so far," he muttered. "She was too ill, too weak."

Deirdre was silent for a moment. "Perhaps she did not wish to be found."

"Why wouldn't she?" Baris demanded, his anger again surfacing. "Why would she hide from me?" He surged to his feet, fists clenched, eyes turned toward the sky.

Deirdre seemed to hesitate before answering, as though she knew what she was about to say might anger him and yet knew also that it must be said. "Baris, she told you to leave. Maybe this is what she wishes, for whatever reason."

He shook his head. "No, she wouldn't do this. Maybe she would run from me but not from Thale. Never from Thale."

Deirdre shrugged. "I have no answers, Baris. But...Thale? Will he live?"

Baris nodded. "Darius says he will. But he needs time to recover. I must leave him in the Lair for now."

"I see. And will you also return to the Lair to be with him?"

"I need to find Anika," he mumbled. He rubbed at his face, then started when Deirdre laid a hand on his arm.

"I agree," she said softly. "But first you need to rest. You'll do Anika no good if you are exhausted." She paused a moment, then added, "Maybe you need to feed. Maybe that would ease your fatigue."

He looked at her, surprised and a little annoyed. "No," he stated flatly. "I don't need to feed. Not yet. I will let you know when I do." He brushed past her to the fire, where he sank down to stare gloomily into the flames.

Deirdre waited a moment, then joined him, though she said nothing more. After a bit, he looked up at her.

"I'm sorry," he said. "I'm not angry at you. I'm just frustrated and upset.

I'm also worried about Anika. I managed to bleed her today, but it was the first time in over a week. I don't know that it was enough. As ill as she is, she might need to be bled more frequently." He got to his feet again, his eyes raking over the lands. "I have to go searching again. I don't have enough magic to shapeshift right now, so it will be on foot. Are you able to travel?"

"Me?" she asked, surprised. "The question is, are you? You need to rest, Baris, have something to eat."

He shook his head. "No, I can't rest. The more I delay, the further away Anika gets. I have to keep going."

Deirdre sighed in resignation. "All right, but at least you need something to drink. I've made some tea. It'll give you some energy. And a few bites of bread won't take that long, will it?"

Baris looked down at her, touched by her concern. He nodded and sat back down. "Very well, a bit of tea and bread, then we must continue on."

"Agreed." She quickly poured out a cupful of tea, then tore a sizeable chunk of bread from a small loaf.

"Did you bring all of this?" Baris asked, taking a sip of the tea.

Deirdre smiled. "I know how men pack. The bare essentials, with nothing included for basic survival."

Baris couldn't help but smile. Already the tea was warming his gut, relaxing him, making his eyelids droop with weariness. Deirdre shook him gently.

"Baris? You can't sleep. I thought we were going to go on?"

Baris rubbed at his eyes, and shook his head to clear it, but his fatigue was too profound. "I fear I have overdone," he told her. "Just a quick nap, then we'll be going. Wake me in ten minutes."

Deirdre nodded, and settled down beside him.

"Ten minutes," he reminded her, and closed his eyes.

He woke some hours later, groggy and disoriented. Deirdre was sitting beside him, her head resting against his chest. It was obvious by the height of the sun that mid-morning was upon him. With a silent curse, he looked down at Deirdre in anger, and shook her awake.

She opened her eyes slowly, as if unwilling to do so, and Baris suddenly realized she must have been as exhausted as he had been. She gasped at the brilliant daylight surrounding her, and spun to face Baris.

"I'm so sorry!" she cried. "I didn't mean to fall asleep! Oh, Baris, I'm..."

He shushed her, his anger snuffed out. Perhaps the little rest would do both of them good. "Seems the head is smarter than the heart," Baris said softly. "I feel better for the sleep. You?"

She nodded, but her face reflected her shame. "I do, but I shouldn't have..."

"Hush," he said, and rose, perusing the mountainous landscape about him. He stared for a long moment, his stomach churning uneasily. If Anika had slipped into the forest, he might never find her. But other things could. Who knew what hungry beasts lived in this rugged land? In her weakened condition, Baris didn't think she would be able to fend off a predator of any size, even using her magic.

"I'm ready to go if you are," Deirdre announced, scrambling to her feet.

Baris smiled at her. "Good. But let me carry the packs." He took them from her, slung them both over his shoulders and they set off, although Baris had no clear idea which way to go. He tried to seek the scent of iron, sure that it would still be strong on Anika, and was puzzled when he could sense nothing. He hadn't taken enough of her blood the previous morning to dampen the iron scent, yet there was absolutely no evidence of it on the morning air.

They walked slowly, calling out Anika's name frequently, listening for any sounds, however feeble, that she might make. There were plenty of animal noises, but no answering call from Anika. Nor could Baris find any traces that she had even passed this direction. Finally, just past noon, he stopped.

"I don't know," he murmured. "Maybe we should have gone the other direction." He looked down at Deirdre. "Can you do anything? Scry for her? Use any of your magic to at least give us a direction?"

The woman frowned. "I don't think so. I told you, I'm not that gifted."

"But you saw Vail and Baul," Baris pointed out. "Why can't you do it again?"

"That was by a large source of water, Baris. I don't have that here."

Baris studied her a moment. "Then we need to find water. There has to be a stream somewhere nearby." He closed his eyes, trying to remember if he had seen anything in his earlier search. But it had been dark and he couldn't recall seeing anything like a lake or a river. Not close by, anyway. With a sigh, he opened his eyes. "Well, we'll just keep on a downhill walk. I guess that's the best we can do for now."

Deirdre didn't argue but followed along silently. They stopped only briefly for a quick lunch before once more setting off. The pair walked at a rapid pace for the remainder of the day. Baris was too lost in his own despair to remember that he far outdistanced Deirdre in both stamina and length of stride. The daylight went quickly, and Baris chastised himself for wasting a good portion of it in his morning nap. Finally, Deirdre tugged at his sleeve, forcing him to stop.

He turned to her in question, then caught his breath. Her face was flushed, her breathing fast. A fine sheen of sweat stood on her brow and she wiped at her face with a kerchief. She lifted her heavy braid off her neck and fanned her skin.

"I'm so sorry," Baris said. "You need to rest."

She nodded, sinking down on a fallen tree. "Just for a bit. I promise.

I'm exhausted. You must be as well."

"No, not yet. But I have pushed you long enough." He pulled the packs from his shoulders and handed them to her. "If you will kindle a fire, I'll see what I can do about dinner."

"I have food," she said. "You don't need to hunt."

Baris watched as she took out several wrapped bundles. He glanced at the skies. They were clear, no clouds marring their expanse. Already the air was cool. It was destined to get colder. And Anika had nothing...no pack, no blankets, no wrap. Just her thin cloak to stand between her and the night's approaching chill. Baris couldn't stand the thought of her being out in the dark, alone, cold and scared.

"Baris." Deirdre's voice was soft, empathetic.

He looked down at her.

"Baris, there's nothing more you can do tonight," she said. "We'll have to wait until it gets light."

He shook his head. "No. After we get a fire going and have something to eat, I'm going to shift. I can keep looking, even in total darkness. I have to find her. She has no protection against the cold."

"I understand." Deirdre began to gather kindling for the fire.

Baris hurried to help her and not much later they had a respectable campfire going. They ate in silence, a meager meal of hard bread, bacon and cheese. Deirdre had brought several small bottles of wine, much to Baris' amusement, and he sipped on the drink, welcoming the warmth it brought to his gut. Finally, he stood up, though his head swirled with the movement. He shook off the dizziness, grimacing. He should have known better than to drink alcohol and then attempt magic. Still, he felt he had no choice in the latter. It was the former he should have avoided.

"Do you have to go?" Deirdre drew a blanket tight about her shoulders as her gaze traveled over the surrounding woods. "I--I'm a little frightened.

I've never been out in the forest at night--alone."

"And what of Anika?" he countered. "She doesn't even have the comfort of a fire." He smiled at her to soften the words. "I won't be gone long. I'm very tired. I don't know how long I can even maintain my shift." He reached out, touched her cheek gently.

She clasped his hand in hers, pressing it against her face. "Hurry back then. And good luck. I hope you find her soon."

He was slow pulling away, confused at the warm emotions of tenderness that raced through him. He quickly shifted again to an owl and took flight. Still, as he flew, his thoughts continually returned to Deirdre. He felt uneasy leaving her alone. He was torn between the need to continue to search for Anika and a desire to return to protect Deirdre. At last, it was no longer his choice.

Dizziness claimed him and he spiraled toward the ground. He had barely enough time to land before he shifted back to Vector form. At that the landing was clumsy and ill-timed. He hit the ground hard, sending shock waves of dull pain through his fatigued body. For a moment, he could do little more than sit and rest, allowing his head to clear, his body to stop shaking. Finally, he rose and slowly made his way back to camp.

Deirdre was sitting close to the fire, her legs pulled up, her blanket wrapped about her like a cocoon. She started at his sudden appearance from the darkness. "You scared me!" she gasped, then frowned. "Are you all right? What happened? Did you see her anywhere?"

"No." He sank down beside the fire, staring forlornly into the flames.

Deirdre hesitated a moment, then moved behind him and began to massage his shoulders. At first, he stiffened in surprise, but soon found himself relaxing into her experienced hands. She worked the taut muscles in his neck, moving her hands in small circles, working her way out to his shoulders, then back. Baris' eyes drooped and he let out a sigh, his thoughts on Anika. Where could she be? Why had she run? Why was she hiding? Or was she hurt, unable to answer?

"While you were gone," Deirdre said softly, "I was thinking what I might do if I was Anika."

"And?"

"I would go to the nearest village, try to find another Vector who could get me inside the Lair. Then I would go in, get Thale and disappear."

The idea startled Baris. "She wouldn't do that," he protested.

"Why not? You said yourself that she wanted you to leave. And she didn't want you to take Thale. So, why wouldn't she decide to leave you instead and take her child with her?"

Baris drew a quick breath. "But she doesn't even know he's there."

"She's not stupid, Baris. She'll figure it out. I mean, where else would you have taken him?"

Baris shook his head, trying to deny the disturbing thoughts her words created. The more he tried, the louder they screamed. He glanced at Deirdre.

"Then tomorrow we, too, will go to the nearest village," he said. "I do not intend to lose my son, Deirdre, not even to Anika."

Chapter Four

Baris woke early, just as the sun was cresting the horizon. Deirdre was already awake. She smiled at him.

"Good morning. I've made some tea," she said.

"Tea?"

"I brought a small pot, remember? It's not going to taste the best, but it'll be welcome. It's rather chilly this morning." She poured some of the amber liquid into a cup and handed it to him.

He wrapped his hands about the mug, savoring the warmth. His gaze went to the campfire and he sighed. He wondered how Anika had fared through the cold night. He wondered if Thale was better. He wondered what the day would hold. Would he find his wife? Would he find out what plagued her? Would Thale recover? Too many questions. He shook them aside and sipped at his tea, letting it warm him inside.

He thought again about Deirdre's words of the previous night. He couldn't imagine Anika seeking out another Vector. She knew the dangers. She knew that being both a witch and a bleeder made her highly sought-after by Vectors. Away from the village, from him, another Vector might choose to lay claim to her. Just the chance of that happening sent daggers of jealousy and alarm through Baris. He couldn't stand the thought of another Vector manipulating her, forcing her to use her magic to supplement his. But more than that, he couldn't stand the thought of another man touching her.

"Baris?"

He started, realizing that Deirdre had been trying to get his attention. She held out a chunk of bread. He shook his head.

"I'm not hungry." He took another sip of his tea. Truthfully, he wasn't thirsty either. But he didn't want to hurt Deirdre's feelings. She had prepared the tea for him. He felt almost duty bound to drink it.

She watched him for a moment. "While you were sleeping, I tried to scry for Anika."

"You did? How?"

"I used some water in a cup. But I wasn't able to conjure an image. I'm sorry."

Baris managed a small smile, touched by her attempt to help. She fidgeted, as if she had more to tell. He waited.

"I didn't get an image," she finally went on. "But I did get a general idea, a sense of a village. I think there's one almost due north of here. Just over these hills. If I could sense it, I'm sure Anika could. She's far more talented."

Hope soared through Baris. He drained his teacup, ignoring the burn of the hot liquid in his throat. "I'll investigate it." He started to stand, intending to shapeshift into a bird.

Deirdre gripped his arm. "No! Don't leave me again. Can't we walk together? I'll keep up, I promise."

Baris hesitated only briefly, then nodded. "Yes, we can walk together." He paused, regarding her carefully, noticing her pallor. "Are you feeling ill?"

She shook her head, then grimaced. "No, not really. But, I think that-- well, maybe tonight, I..." She broke off, flushing.

Baris brushed her hair from her face, understanding what she was trying to say. She needed to be bled. She had used magic, and even though Baris couldn't really sense the iron on her, he didn't doubt her own self-analysis.

"Tonight then, Deirdre," he said softly. "I don't want you to get ill as well. And you are ill because of me."

She flashed him a smile of gratitude then swiftly broke camp. They were on the trail within the quarter-hour. Deirdre linked her arm through his in an effort to keep stride with him. Baris slowed his pace, guilt over the previous day fresh in his mind. Still, two hours later, Deirdre was panting.

"Shall we stop?" he asked.

"No, that's all right. I promised I would keep up."

He smiled. "And fall over in a faint trying to. Let's try something different." He stepped back away from her, used his Vector magic and shapeshifted into a stallion.

Deirdre gasped, her eyes brightening. "Oh, my," was all she could manage.

Baris tossed his head and huffed out a small breath, encouraging her to climb onto his back. He was a little surprised at how the shift had affected him. Usually it went easily, but this time he felt drained, as if he had already used a great deal of his magic.

Deirdre took up the pack and climbed onto his back. She twisted one hand into his mane. With the other, she stroked his neck. The touch sent pleasant shivers through him. He snorted softly and started out at a smooth walk. He didn't have the energy for much else.

It was nearing dusk when his keen hearing picked up the sound of running water. He turned toward it at once, not only to slake his thirst but hoping that Deirdre could use it for her magic. They found a wide, rushing river not long after. Deirdre slid from Baris' back and hurried to the bank while Baris shifted back to Vector form. He swayed dizzily and grabbed at a nearby tree to support himself. For a moment, darkness hovered before his eyes. Worry began to gnaw at his gut. For the first time, he began to wonder if what Anika had was contagious. Was he now starting to show symptoms of some human ailment? And more importantly, would Thale become ill as well? Should Baris return to the Lair to check on the boy? Or would such a visit only serve to infect Thale if he wasn't already sick? And what of the other Vectors? It was rare for a Vector to become ill. If he was experiencing a human illness, it meant there might be no protection from it. He could well destroy the entire Lair. No, better to wait it out, see what happened to him first. When the dizziness passed, he sought out Deirdre.

She was on her knees, leaning over the water, staring intently into its swirling depths. Baris' heart did an unexpected twist. Her eagerness to help warmed him. No wonder Holt was so enamored with her. With a sigh, Baris knelt behind her, peering over her shoulder into the water.

He was surprised to see a faint image floating on the river's surface. "That's Vail!" he gasped. "Isn't it?"

Deirdre nodded, though she said nothing.

"Can you talk to him? Can you find out where he is?"

"I'm trying," she murmured.

Baris fell silent, not wanting to break her concentration. Only when the image faded did he speak again. "Well? Did you find out where he is?"

Deirdre sat back, a weary sigh escaping her. "I think so. If I understood him right, he's in a village by the name of Erster. Have you ever heard of it?"

Baris frowned. "No, I don't think so. Did it seem far away from here? Farther than Nowles?"

"I can't judge distance through a vision," Deirdre told him.

"The village that you sensed earlier, are we close? Do you know the name of it?"

She shook her head. "I'm sorry."

Baris took her by the shoulders and turned her around to face him. "You keep saying that. You have nothing to be sorry for, Deirdre. I appreciate your help." He stroked her hair gently, as he might a child in his care who sought reassurance. "And your companionship." He glanced through the forest canopy at the darkening skies. "We can probably walk another few hours, if you're up to it."

She nodded and rose. "I would like to find this village. Sleeping on the ground isn't my favorite pastime."

Baris chuckled. "Oh, so, you wish to see the world, but in style?"

Deirdre giggled. "All right. I'm no woods-woman, I admit it. I do like my comfort."

"So do I," Baris admitted, straightening. "I'll bet if we follow the river, it'll take us right into town."

"Sounds reasonable," she agreed. "But you won't shift again?"

He shook his head, not comfortable with explaining his sudden weakness. "I'll just walk for a bit. I thought you might like conversation, something I can't do in animal shape."

She smiled at him. "Yes, that would be nice. Although, you make a fine stallion."

He flushed at the gentle teasing, took up the pack and once more led the way. And although he had intended on conversation during the walk, he found himself too exhausted to do so. Still, Deirdre didn't seem to mind, and they traveled in an easy silence, reaching the village long after dark. Baris took a moment to shape-shift, this time to an older man that might be taken for Deirdre's father at a quick glance. Together, he and she wearily climbed the stairs of the only inn. Baris went to the counter while Deirdre sank down on a bench near the fire.

The innkeeper approached with a broad smile on his jowled face. "What can I do you for?"

"A room, please," Baris said, then added, "one for each of us."

The man glanced over at Deirdre, and a frown crinkled his face. "Two rooms?" he murmured. The innkeeper paused, his gaze still on Deirdre. "I-- only have one room left," he mumbled. "The others are all full." He gave a slight shiver as if a chill had caught at him, then brought his gaze back to Baris. "I can send up a cot if you like, but that's the best I can do for tonight. Perhaps by tomorrow night, some of the other guests will have left and I can move you into a separate room."

Baris grimaced, but not because he was unwilling to share a room. He trusted himself, his morals, his bond to Anika. Still, he certainly didn't want to give Anika any support for her ideas about his 'relationship' with Deirdre. On the other hand, sleeping in the barn just didn't sound like a pleasant way to end an exhausting day. He nodded. "Very well. A cot will suffice. Thank you."

"Pay on your way out, then." The innkeeper slid a key to Baris. "You look like a trustworthy fellow." He turned and disappeared into the back.

Baris glanced at the room number engraved on the key and beckoned Deirdre to follow. "He only had one room. I hope you don't mind. I did ask him to send up a cot. You may have the bed."

She smiled. "I don't mind sharing. I'm glad you didn't think you had to sleep in the barn."

Baris started, then chuckled. "Those were my thoughts exactly." He led the way up the wide, wooden staircase and down a narrow hallway to the room.

It was cold and dark inside, and Baris quickly put a flame to a lantern from the wall sconces in the hallway. It took a bit more work to get a respectable fire going, but at last he succeeded. He stood warming his hands before the flame.

Deirdre collapsed onto the wide bed with a sigh of relief. "It feels good to have a real bed again."

Baris chuckled. "Only one night outside and already you're tired of it? How will you survive seeing the world at this rate?"

She giggled. "I came prepared. I brought my entire dowry with me." She hefted her pack.

Baris heard the clink of coin. He smiled. "A teapot, money--what else did you bring with you?"

"Just my desires," she answered.

Baris felt his smile freeze, although his heart pounded in sudden anticipation. "Your--desires?"

Deirdre blushed. "To see the world, Baris. What did you think I meant?"

He shook his head, chastising himself, then turned to the sideboard. "I'm going to get some water to wash with."

"All right. Would you like me to make some tea when you get back?"

He nodded and quickly left the room. Once in the hallway, he took a moment to compose himself. What was wrong with him? He couldn't believe what had just happened. For just a brief moment, he had actually felt a sharp flame of lust for Deirdre. And earlier, when she had touched him, he had experienced a rush of desire. Did his vows to Anika mean nothing? Perhaps she was right after all. Perhaps he had mistaken lust for love and now was being drawn to a new, more exciting woman without even being aware of it. Had Anika seen it, recognized his straying attention? Had it been her unspoken grief over his emotional desertion that had brought on her illness?

No, he couldn't believe that. He loved Anika, needed her, wanted her. Only her. He was just tired and upset. He shook his head and went in search of the water.

When he returned, he felt more in control, but that swiftly left him when he saw how Deirdre was clothed. She stood before the hearth, the light from the fire piercing straight through her long white nightgown. Her generously curved body was perfectly outlined. Baris stood just inside the doorway, one hand gripping the doorknob, the other the pitcher of water. She turned to him, smiling, then shook out her hair so that it rippled over her shoulders, falling to either side of her full, round breasts. Baris swallowed hard and set the water down on the nearest table with a thud.

Deirdre's smile faded. "What's wrong? You don't look well."

"N...no," Baris stammered. "I'm fine. Really." He massaged his temples gently. His head was suddenly pounding as hard as his heart. He forced his gaze from her breasts, and looked into her eyes. "Deirdre, I don't think this is a good idea. Sharing a room, I mean."

"Why not?" she asked, her tone innocent. "The only thing safer than sharing a room with a happily married man is sharing a room with your own brother."

Baris managed to pull his gaze away from her, angered at his body's response to her sensuality. "Still, I think it would be best if I bed down in the barn."

"That's silly!" she protested. "Besides, I'm not sure I would feel comfortable being here alone. You make me feel protected. And besides, you did promise to bleed me tonight. Remember?"

Baris had forgotten. He barely managed to contain his moan of despair.

He was already reacting to her presence. It would only get more intense if he bled her. He forced his thoughts to Anika, disgusted with himself for his lack of control. He shook his head.

"Not tonight, Deirdre," he said firmly. "I...I need to go out. I will inform the innkeeper that you are here alone and have him make certain you are safe. You can bolt the door as well. The room is on the second floor. No one should be able to gain entry through a window, but you should bolt that as well. There's enough wood to last the night. Order up whatever you wish for dinner. I will find my own. You will be fine."

"But Baris, you..."

"No! Not tonight, Deirdre. Please." Without another word, he snatched up his cloak and bolted from the room.

He didn't slow his pace until he was in the dark streets, well away from the inn. It didn't even occur to him that he hadn't stopped to talk to the innkeeper as he'd said he would. He had suddenly been so desperate to simply get away from Deirdre, from the temptation she so inexplicably now presented, that he could think of nothing else.

Except his need to feed. She had been right about that. He was feeling the urge more strongly than he had in a long time. It was probably because he had gone without for so long. What he had taken from Anika two days ago had only served to whet his appetite.

Irritation pricked him. He had the perfect source to relieve his hunger and he wasn't making use of it. Deirdre needed to be bled; he needed the blood she offered. He should be strong enough to feed without wanting more from her. The love he felt for Anika should make him strong enough.

The irritation turned to annoyance as he strode through the dark streets, not really conscious of his surroundings. He forced his thoughts away from Deirdre, from the temptation of Deirdre, to Thale. Was his son recovering? Or was he now sick with whatever ailed Anika? Would Anika indeed try to get to him, remove him from the Lair with the help of some other Vector, offer her blood, her body, just to deprive Baris of his child? And if she did, would she then disappear with Thale?

Pain sliced into Baris' heart. No. He wouldn't let her do that. He loved his son with a passion he hadn't known he possessed. He couldn't live not knowing where Thale was. He had told Darius nothing about Anika's behavior, though why he wasn't sure. True, it was no secret that the Vector Sovereign would have preferred that Vector and human not marry. He had not protested much when Jaeger had taken Rhiannon as his wife, but then again Jaeger was half-human. Baris was not. He was full Vector and, though he had been created from the prior Sovereign's seed, that made no difference to Darius. Baris was a Vector and he was bound by the reigning Sovereign's rule.

Why he had even been allowed to wed Anika he didn't know. He suspected he had caught Darius in a rare mood of flexibility. However, after their union, Darius had stopped any further intermarriages. He had cited the mortality factor; the emotional needs of humans that Vectors didn't share, the fact that a continuing pattern of intermarriages could condemn the Vector race to annihilation if too many mixed families denied their children the means of achieving their Vector heritage.

Still, Darius had never shown any animosity toward Anika. Or toward Thale. He seemed to care for the child much the way a proud grandfather would. And had shown it by taking in Thale without question. Would he then stand aside and allow Anika access to her son? Or would he stop her? Question her?

Baris needed to speak further with Darius, to talk to the Vector Sovereign about his dilemma, to make sure that Anika was not given the opportunity to spirit the child away. But first, he needed strength. And for that he needed blood.

He stopped walking, taking in his surroundings. His blind steps had taken him to the village's tavern district. Drunken men stumbled through the streets, pawing at whores who giggled and staggered with them into run-down inns. Thieves stole through the shadows, rifling the pockets of those dropped by drink. The thought of taking blood from one of the drunks or whores disgusted him. And most of the thieves were not much more savory-looking. Most were probably diseased, as well. With a heavy sigh, he turned back toward the inn. He would be quick, he told himself. And professional. He would take only what blood he needed to both regain his own strength and to ease her illness. And that was all he would take. It had to be.

Chapter Five

He found Deirdre asleep in the chair before the hearth. The firelight played over her dark locks and creamy complexion, but memories of Anika strengthened Baris' resolution. His heart ached for his beloved, ached to know where she was, in what condition. He vowed he would search for her again tomorrow. The longer she went without being bled, the more powerful the scent of iron would be. He should be able to find her on that alone.

He hung his cloak and approached the hearth quietly. A teapot simmered on the crank, emitting enticing spicy aromas. Baris picked up a cloth and poured a mug of the amber liquid. It burned a path to his stomach, but took the chill from his body. There was no cot. Apparently the best the innkeeper could do was a wide divan, placed tantalizingly close to the bed. Baris moved it away, drawing it quietly up beside the chair

Deirdre slumbered in. He sagged onto the divan and watched Deirdre sleep, as he sipped at the tea.

The beverage left his tongue tingling, his throat soothed yet begging for more. He downed what he had left and poured another cupful, then sat back to brood again on the change that had come over his wife. He ransacked his memory for what he might have said or done to trigger it, some event that could have affected her without his being aware, but he couldn't place the blame on any one thing. Not even himself. He had always been faithful, loving, thoughtful. At least, he thought he had. Perhaps Anika had seen him in a different way. Something had obviously brought about her change of heart.

Up until about five months ago, she had been her usual warm and loving self. She and Baris had been exquisitely happy. They had even talked of adding another child to their family. Their shared passion for Thale reflected their passion for each other. They could barely keep their hands off one another.

Now? It was as if there was an icy chasm between them, with no bridge in sight. Baris didn't want to lose Anika. Yet, he couldn't bear the idea of staying with her the way it was. Something had to change.

His gaze drifted again to Deirdre. She shifted slightly and her gown fell open, exposing her long, white, slender neck and chest. Baris took a long drink of his tea, averting his gaze, but it crept back as if of its own accord. His breath quickened as his body responded to her closeness, her scent. He could now smell the iron on her. She was right. She did need to be bled. With a trembling hand he leaned forward, stretched his long arm out and touched her.

She came awake with a start, then smiled dreamily upon seeing him. "I'm glad you came back," she whispered.

"So am I," he replied, pulling back. He finished off the tea and set his cup aside, tipping his head at the teapot. "That was very good. Was it a special blend?"

She smiled slowly and nodded. "One I made up. It's wonderful for chasing the chill from your bones." Her voice was deep, sultry. Or was he only imagining it?

"Indeed it is." He smiled at her apologetically, forcing aside the urge to touch her further. "Deirdre, I came back for a reason. You said you needed to be bled after using your magic earlier. I need your blood. I would like to return to the Lair and talk further with Darius about Thale and Anika. I don't have the magical strength to do that right now."

"It's yours for the taking," she told him, sitting up straighter. Her gown slid down her shoulders, almost baring her breasts.

Baris swallowed hard, forcing his gaze away. He was not quite sure how to go about the whole procedure. He had promised himself that he would be quick and professional, but just the thought of touching her was sending chills racing through him. And her state of semi-nudity was unsettling to say the least. She must have guessed his uneasiness, for she rose, pulled her gown closed, and settled next to him on the chaise. She tossed her hair aside and grinned.

He stared at her, hoping that she wouldn't notice the shallow quickness of his breathing. As much as he chastised himself, he couldn't control the way his body was betraying him. Slowly, he put one arm around her, shivering at the smooth softness of her skin. Her cheeks were aglow, her eyes no less, sparkling in the firelight. She was radiantly beautiful and Baris reached his other hand to touch her silken tresses.

Quick and professional, his mind screamed. Take her, his body argued.

With a sharp intake of breath, he pulled her close and bit into her neck. Her blood was unlike anything he had ever tasted. It filled his senses, made him both hot and cold at the same time, set him trembling with desire. She leaned into him with a small gasp, wrapping her arms about his neck, tangling her fingers into his dark hair, pressing against him. Each little pull of his locks sent pain and pleasure vying for attention in Baris' mind.

He didn't want to let her go, yet finally he forced himself back and away, his heart racing, his blood pounding in his ears. She frowned at him, confused.

"What's wrong?"

He shook his head, reeling. "I don't know. I'm just dizzy. It's nothing, I'm sure." He adjusted his clothing, embarrassed by his obvious desire to have her. "Deirdre, I--I didn't mean for this--well, I didn't mean--"

She shushed him with one long finger to his lips. "I know. I understand a lot more than you think. It's between you and me. Anika will never know."

Mention of his wife brought his guilt back. By the Sovereign! What had he been thinking? He had never been unfaithful, never betrayed his wife before. Why should he now harbor such thoughts? Was he that angry with her? That desperate for someone to fill her place? Was he really that much of a Vector that he couldn't keep his thoughts and emotions centered on one woman? He rose, self-recrimination hammering at him. Again, he staggered dizzily, then collapsed onto the bed, sleep pulling at him.

He had wanted to do something, but he couldn't remember what. He was just so dreadfully tired all of a sudden. He needed to sleep. He couldn't concentrate when he was so tired. His need for rest seemed to overpower everything else.

"If you're going to sleep," Deirdre said softly. "Then do it right."

She pulled his tunic over his head, then pulled back the covers on the bed. He rolled onto his back, the cool freshness of the sheets welcome on his hot skin, as she tugged off his boots.

"Your breeches should come off as well," Deirdre said with a small smile. "Otherwise, they'll not be fit to travel in tomorrow."

"No," he said at once. "No, I--I think I'd better leave them on."

She shrugged. "Suit yourself. I'll be sleeping on the divan anyway."

"No," he protested weakly. "You should have the bed." He tried to rise but could not seem to get his body to obey.

Deirdre merely smiled and moved away. "It makes more sense this way, Baris. I'm the smaller of us. Good night, and thank you."

She moved out of his range of sight and Baris fell into a deep, exhausted sleep.

He woke the next morning with a roaring head and a sick stomach. His thoughts were scattered and confused. But when his gaze fell on the woman lying beside him, snugged against his side, cheek pressed against his bare chest, his memories returned with a sickening rush. He bolted from the bed as if the bedclothes were on fire, wakening Deirdre in the process. She looked up at him with sleepy eyes.

"I'm sorry," she mumbled. "I got cold. The fire went out."

Baris' gaze flew to the cold hearth. He stumbled toward it and threw some wood and kindling on. With shaking hands, he coaxed it to flame, and it gradually took the chill from the room. Deirdre watched from the bed, her gown hugging her body, outlining every delicious curve. Baris averted his gaze, his mouth going dry.

"Now, if I could have done that--" she said, pointing at the fire with a smile.

Baris crouched on one knee and peered into the teapot. It was empty. He glanced over at Deirdre. "Think you could brew up some more tea? I could use it. I'm feeling a bit unsettled this morning. I'll go down and arrange breakfast."

She nodded, climbing from the bed. Her gown was unlaced at the top and fell open to both sides, again almost exposing her breasts, although she seemed not to notice. Baris swallowed hard, got back on his feet and reached for his tunic. He slipped it on, tied the sash and with one last glance at Deirdre, left the room.

Outside, in the dark hallway, he took a moment to compose himself. He raked his fingers through his unruly dark hair and rubbed at his face. Guilt tormented him. What had he done? Anything? Nothing? He couldn't remember. All he knew was that he had wakened with Deirdre in his arms. Had he made love to her? No. He shook his head. He would know, wouldn't he? By the Sovereign! Perhaps he had no right to try to win back Anika after his behavior last night. After what might have happened during the dark hours. He couldn't keep such a secret from her. If he ever found her and they returned home, he would confess everything before Deirdre or someone else could tell her. Would she forgive him, understand that it had meant nothing, that he had been driven by his exhaustion and his need for magic to find her? Or would she order him once again to leave her?

And what of Thale? Had Darius spoken the truth that he would recover, or was he lost as well? That thought left Baris weak-kneed and trembling. He Illusioned himself and stumbled down the stairs to the front counter, where the innkeeper was already at work.

"Good morn, sir," the man greeted him, with a smile. The smile faded when he took in Baris' complexion. Apparently, even the illusion couldn't completely disguise his condition. "My goodness! You look ill, sir. Might I fetch you a healer?"

Baris shook his head, sending little daggers of pain shooting through it. "No, I'm fine. But I would like to order breakfast. Bread, eggs, a bit of bacon or beef, if you have it." He paused, as his stomach rumbled loudly.

"Make it ample. I'm quite hungry."

"Tea?"

"No. My companion prepares her own. Thank you." Baris turned and dragged himself back up the stairs. The effort was exhausting. He barely made it to the room.

Deirdre looked up at him as he staggered inside and collapsed on the bed. She approached with a worried countenance and a steaming mug of tea. "Here, this should soothe you."

He propped himself up and accepted the tea with shaking hands. The first sip was welcome. It coated his mouth and tongue, slid easily down his stinging throat, swirled through his stomach leaving it warm and comforted. He leaned his head back against the headboard with a sigh.

"Thank you, Deirdre," he murmured. "I don't know what's gotten into me." He took another sip, relishing the relief it provided. "How do you know how to brew these different teas?"

She shrugged, perching on the edge of the bed near his feet. "I study. And I experiment. I have to admit that some of my experiments haven't turned out so well." She giggled as if remembering some of the worst.

Baris smiled. "Well, I thank you for discovering this particular one. It's doing the trick. My stomach feels better already and my headache is starting to fade as well. I wasn't sure that I would be able to continue my search for Anika today but now I think I will."

For a moment Deirdre stiffened, then she sighed. "I can't imagine where she would have gone to. This is the closest village, yet I didn't see her anywhere."

"See her? When did you go looking?"

"Last eve, after you left. I tried scrying for her again."

"Then that's why you were so tired! You used more magic. Deirdre, I am very grateful, but I don't want you to make yourself sick trying to find

Anika. This is my problem, not yours. You are along for the adventure, nothing more."

She grinned at him, tipping her head to reveal the two small bite marks on her neck. "Nothing more?"

He felt the color rush to his face. "All right, I concede to that. After a look at the citizens of this village, I wouldn't trust anyone but you. I would have been a fool to reject your offer." He paused, then added. "But, I must apologize for my actions. I am sorry."

"Don't apologize, Baris," Deirdre said quietly. "Nothing happened."

The words sent a wave of relief through Baris. He watered it with another long sip of the pungent tea.

"And besides, " Deirdre went on. "An apology makes me feel--well, ugly."

He gasped. "Ugly! You are far from that, Deirdre! Very far. You are exquisitely beautiful. It's no wonder that Holt is so taken with you."

She grimaced. "Please, don't mention Holt."

Baris paused. "He is your betrothed, is he not?"

"No! Not yet, anyway. And if I have my way about it, he never will be. I will not be sold to any man."

"Sold? I hardly think you were sold."

"What's the difference?" she demanded. "My father offered me to Holt as if I were no more than a commodity, another sheep or goat to fatten Holt's herd. And he accepted me as such. I will not become just another piece of property to Holt. I won't."

Baris studied her thoughtfully. "I don't know a lot about clan custom, that's true," he said. "But I don't agree with forcing any woman to marry someone she does not love." A heavy sigh escaped him. "And I am perhaps to blame for just that. I may have forced Anika into this marriage. She may not have wanted me at all. I was so entranced with her, with her beauty both inside and out, that I possessed her. I may have even used my Vector magic. I don't know anymore."

Deirdre looked over at him, her eyes wide with innocent confusion. "Your magic?"

"Yes. I can use it to enslave a person's will. That's often how Vectors attain their..." He broke off. He didn't want to say 'victims', but he couldn't think of another word for it. He shook his head and drained the tea from his mug, then looked up as a knock sounded at the door. "Ah, that must be breakfast. And just in time. I'm starved." He rose from the bed, opened the door and accepted the breakfast tray from the serving wench.

The aroma of fresh eggs and sausage filled the room and set his stomach rumbling. He closed the door and placed the tray on the sidetable, then motioned Deirdre forward. She joined him eagerly.

"This smells wonderful! But why so much? Are you really that hungry?"

He chuckled. "I don't know. It seemed so this morning. And I want you to regain your strength as well. Eat hearty. We have some walking to do today. But directly after breakfast, I am going to the Lair. I want to check on Thale and discuss Anika with Darius."

Deirdre turned to him. "But that will deplete your magic won't it? Wouldn't it be better to use that magic to find Anika? Thale is in good hands, you know that. And I would suppose that someone would fetch you straightaway if he took a turn for the worse."

Baris met her gaze, puzzled that she seemed to be trying to persuade him not to go. Yet, the moment he looked into her eyes, he realized she made considerable sense. Plus there was the slim chance that if the boy wasn't already infected with Anika's illness, Baris could take it to him. He nodded. "Yes, I suppose you're right. And Thale probably needs rest more than anything else. Thank you, Deirdre. You seem to be able to sort out my confused state of mind. Let's eat. Then we can start our search for Anika anew."

She nodded, gave him a small smile and dished up her food.

Chapter Six

They left the inn later that morning. The sun was shining and the air was crisp, which gave Baris a strange sense of well-being. He took a deep breath of the fresh mountain air as they walked along the main street and smiled at Deirdre. He noticed at once that she was shivering.

"We need to get you a proper cloak," he said. "That one you have on is more suited for the lowlands than up here in the mountains."

"It's fine. I don't want to waste my money on such extravagances."

He looped one of his arms through hers. "Then we'll waste mine," he told her and led her to a shop across the wide dirt street.

Inside it was warm and cozy. The shelves were lined with all sorts of apparel from cloaks to nightwear. Sturdy boots lined one wall, while hats of various shapes and material hung on pegs above. Deirdre went at once to the hats, while Baris perused the selection of heavy wool cloaks.

He shook out a dark red one, holding it up, picturing how it would look with Deirdre's dark hair lying against it. As he did so, his eye caught on a royal blue wrap. Slowly, he laid the red one aside and picked up the blue one. Blue. It was Anika's favorite color. It brought out the glacial blue of her eyes like no other color. By the Sovereign, how he missed gazing into those eyes.

With a heavy sigh, he replaced the blue cloak, reclaimed the red and turned toward Deirdre. A smile touched his lips. She had placed a wool hat atop her dark curls and was examining her reflection in a small mirror hanging on one wall. The hat was a reddish color, sporting a variety of feathery plumes in brilliant white. A piece of embossed red leather circled the crown of the hat. It was imprinted with bird designs, each bird's tail plumage touching the next bird's beak. It was garish and bright, yet at the same time it looked sexily appropriate on Deirdre. Carefully avoiding the mirror and his lack of reflection in it, Baris joined her.

"It looks wonderful," he said.

She blushed and took the hat off. "It's far too loud."

"It looks wonderful," he repeated firmly, then held out the cloak. "Here, try this on." He slipped it over her shoulders and tied it beneath her chin. "The collar is satin, so it won't chafe your neck or chin."

She reached up to stroke the soft material at her nape, then looked into the mirror. "It's beautiful, Baris, but it's quite costly, is it not?"

"Don't worry over that." He took the hat from her and placed it back on her head. "And it looks fabulous with the hat."

She appraised herself in the mirror. "Do you think so?"

"I do, indeed." He turned toward the merchant, who had been watching them silently. "I think we'll take both. She'll wear them."

"Both?" Deirdre gasped. "But, Baris, the cost!"

He waved her protests away and eyed the merchant, who was now grinning widely, apparently expecting to hear the clink of coin into his outstretched palm. Instead, Baris gazed into the man's eyes. It took only a moment to convince the merchant that no payment was necessary, and his hand dropped limply to the countertop. Baris was aware of Deirdre's eyebrows rising in--what? Surprise? Awe? Delight?

Baris took her by the elbow and steered her toward the door. Once outside, he rolled her old cloak and stuffed it into his pack. It would make an extra layer in case they found themselves without the benefit of an inn. He glanced up and down the street. Neither of them spoke about the incident that had just occurred.

"Well, since you scryed for Anika last eve and she wasn't here," Baris said, "I suggest we move on toward Nowles. I can take council with Jaeger and Rhiannon. Perhaps they can use their magic to find her. Once we are out of the village, I will shapeshift so you don't have to walk the entire day. Breakfast and rest have restored my strength."

"Mine as well. I don't mind walking. I fear I indulged too much in breakfast. The walk will do me good."

He laughed and started down the street in the direction they had come the night before.

"This Illusion you've created," Deirdre said, gesturing at his body as they walked. "Why such an old man?"

Baris shrugged. "I thought it would be best. I wouldn't want to spoil any attention you might garner from a local young man."

Deirdre wrinkled her nose. "And who says I wish attention from any young man? Besides, they might all stay away, thinking you're my father."

Baris chuckled. "Then what should I look like?"

"Well, I would wish you could appear as yourself, without having to use an Illusion, but I know that's not safe." She sighed, glancing up at him from the corner of her eye. "So--how about a handsome younger man? Someone I would be proud to be seen with, instead of a dotty old man?"

"Dotty?" Baris lifted his eyebrows in amusement. "I am not dotty."

She grinned. "Well, maybe not dotty, but certainly old. So, next Illusion, do I get a younger man?"

"I'll think about it. Even if I'll then likely have to fight off your potential suitors."

Deirdre laughed again, and a short time later they left the small village for the forest. The walk was invigorating, filled with laughter and conversation. Baris had to actually remind himself of his goal...that he was searching for Anika. When that happened, he couldn't believe how easily she had slipped from his mind. It was disconcerting and puzzling. Still, Deirdre's bubbly chatter seemed to keep his despair at bay, which wasn't necessarily a bad thing; and by lunchtime, he was in almost a jovial mood himself.

They stopped beside a shallow brook to rest and eat. Baris was amazed at the way rest, proper food and blood had restored his mood and strength. He was feeling almost normal again.

"If you could build the fire while I prepare lunch, it will save a little time," Deirdre said.

Baris willingly gathered the kindling. It didn't take him long to have a respectable flame going. Deirdre filled the teapot with water from the stream and set it to boil. She gestured at the stream. "Would you like me to try scrying again?"

Baris started, realizing it was the first time in several hours that Anika had crossed his mind. He frowned. He wished he could talk to Deirdre about these peculiar lapses in focus, but found the idea of confessing them somewhat embarrassing. What kind of man would forget about his own wife, knowing she was ill and lost? Was it possible she meant that little to him? And if she did, then why was he bothering to pursue her? Why not let her go? It was what she had said she wanted, and she was an adult. Surely she knew her own mind and heart. Why should he not simply go on himself?

He shook his head as though to drive the treacherous thoughts away and a familiar ache touched his heart. He *did* love Anika. He had loved her the moment he'd set eyes on her. And he did want to find her. He would not believe she truly wanted him gone from her life, not until he was certain she was well and in her right mind. He sighed and looked at the water.

"Do you think you'll be able to get a vision of her? If not, I don't want you to use your magic. It just makes you ill."

"I won't know unless I try," Deirdre said, rising. "No, you stay here. I work better alone."

Baris nodded and watched her move to the stream. She knelt beside it and bent over the water. Baris rubbed wearily at his face, got up and walked into the forest to attend to personal matters. The air was cool, the light dim. He wondered where Anika was, how she was surviving. She'd had nothing...no blankets, no food, no water. For the first time in hours, true despair clutched at Baris and he hurried back to the encampment to see what Deirdre had found. Without thinking he strode up next to her at the stream. A vision in the water immediately disappeared as she gasped, startled at his sudden appearance.

"That looked like Vail," he said.

"It...it was," she stammered. "I managed to locate him. I told him we were on our way to Nowles and asked him to meet us there."

"And Anika? Were you able to find her?"

Deirdre shook her head and climbed to her feet. "No. She must be using her magic to block mine. I truly don't think she wants to be found."

"It's beginning to look that way," Baris admitted reluctantly. Tears stung his eyes and he tipped his head back to gaze into the noon sky. "Why? Why would she do that? Does she truly despise me so much? She'll take Thale, I know it." He thought again about going to the Lair, just to be sure Thale was all right, to warn Darius that Anika might try to steal the boy away. And just as quickly the thought slipped away when Deirdre touched him.

She slipped her hand into his and squeezed gently. "Come, let's have something to eat. I'm sure Jaeger will be able to help you once we get to Nowles."

He allowed her to lead him back to the fire, where he slumped to the hard ground. Deirdre poured him a mug of tea, then laid out a simple meal of bread and cheese. Baris sipped his tea, watching her. He wondered about her relationship with Holt, if she truly did dislike him. Or was she only expressing her reluctance to be married and tied down while she was still so young?

Thoughts of Holt left a bitter taste in Baris' mouth. It was bad enough that Holt should treat Deirdre as a possession, but worse that he should give her a time frame in which to return to him. The thought that he would then hunt her down was repulsive. Baris wouldn't let Holt drag her back to the village unless Deirdre truly wanted to go. And he was quite certain she didn't.

The issue of Holt settled, Baris relaxed as the tea warmed his gut and calmed his anxiety over Anika's lengthening absence. Sunlight stole through the forest canopy and sent rainbows of color through Deirdre's hair. Baris had the sudden urge to touch it, to let his fingers caress its softness. He shook the thought away and ate his lunch in silence. Guilt tore at him, yet at the same time, he wanted to be with Deirdre. He couldn't understand his confused emotions.

It warmed his heart how she was trying so hard to help him find Anika. But there was more to his feelings than that. He had to be honest and admit he was drawn to her as a man to a woman. He liked her, found her engaging and fun to be around. Still, he had never in his married life entertained such thoughts for another woman. Was he doing so now because deep down he believed Anika had set him free?

He cringed at the very thought. Set him free? As if he had been trapped, enslaved? He hadn't. He loved Anika. He loved Thale. He wanted them to be a family again. He wanted things back the way they had been, though he had begun to fear they never could be. Not when his mind and his body were straying to another woman, a woman he had actually shared a bed with.

True, Deirdre said nothing had happened, but Baris knew in his gut that it had been very close. He had wanted Deirdre with every fiber of his being. His body ached for her even now, remembered how hers had felt against his. How could he go back to living in the same village with her, even if they found Anika and cured whatever afflicted her? His feelings of lust were unlikely to disappear and at some point someone would be sure to notice. Then Anika would know and once that happened she would be well within her rights to leave him and take Thale with her. The thought tore Baris up inside and he could no longer sit still. He finished off his tea and handed the mug back to Deirdre, then got to his feet.

"We need to keep moving," he said. "Even at a brisk pace, it will take us two more days to get to Nowles. I need to shift into something that can give us that brisk pace."

Deirdre sighed but nodded. "I just hate the silence," she explained. "If I could converse with you while you are in animal form, it would be so much nicer."

"I'm sorry. I wish that were possible." He winced at her crestfallen look. His need to please her seemed strangely important to him. "How about a compromise then? I promise you that I won't spend more than half of each day in animal form. How's that?"

She smiled up at him and finished packing away the remnants of their lunch. "That sounds like an equitable exchange." She came to stand next to him, then looked toward the stream. "Would you like me to scry one more time before we move on? Just in case she's close by someplace?"

Baris paused, his gaze moving over the countryside as if he expected to see his wife step from the shrubbery. "What good would it do?" he sighed. "If she is blocking your magic, you still would not find her."

"But even Anika has to sleep," Deirdre pointed out. "And when she does, her magic shields will either drop or not be as effective. I might be able to sense her, at least. Let me try. Please."

He regarded her thoughtfully. "If you use magic, you will need to be bled again."

She averted her gaze, color rushing to her cheeks. "I'm sorry. I don't want to push you into something you find uncomfortable. I only thought that..."

He reached out and drew her close, wishing only to ease her obvious upset. "Uncomfortable? No, Deirdre, I do not find it uncomfortable. In fact, I may be finding it a little too comfortable. I told you that it was sometimes difficult to separate the...emotional...side of feeding from the physical act."

Still smiling, she placed one cool hand on his cheek. "I promise I'll be good," she said softly. She gently moved away from him to kneel down at stream's edge.

Baris suppressed a sigh. Good? You're not just good, he told her silently. You're sinfully exquisite.

They reached the small village of Terska just after dark. Baris wasn't taken with the unkempt streets or rundown buildings. Still, a room at the solitary inn would be preferable to sleeping on the ground in the cold, mountain air. He kept Deirdre close to his side as they walked. Whether it was her beauty or her expensive clothing that was garnering the attention Baris didn't know, but he wasn't going to take chances he didn't need to.

As per Deirdre's request, after having spent the morning as a horse, he had now shapeshifted to a young man. He was glad of it. His size and appearance might prove sufficiently intimidating to those leering men watching them. Nevertheless, he was relieved when he and Deirdre finally arrived at the inn. They slipped inside, closing the battered door against all further gawking.

"Kin I help you?" The innkeeper hefted his bulky frame from a sagging chair behind a littered, and dirty counter.

"Yes. We'd like two..." Baris was interrupted by Deirdre's gasp of dismay. He looked down at her.

"Do I have to stay alone?" she whispered.

Baris hesitated, remembering the dangers of being in such close quarters with her. Still, the fear in her dark eyes was daunting and he finally shook his head, patting her hand gently.

"No. I quite understand." He looked back at the innkeeper. "One room, please. If you have a cot I would like one sent up as well."

The innkeeper looked from Baris to Deirdre, where his gaze lingered for a long moment. Then a slight grin curved the man's mouth, and he took a key from underneath the counter. He shoved it at Baris, all the while watching Deirdre, his lust obvious. It was hard for Baris to keep from laying the man flat. Instead, he snatched up the key and escorted Deirdre up the sagging stairway and down a dimly lit hallway.

They found their room quickly; and, once inside, Baris bolted the door. Deirdre put down her pack, wrapped her arms about her chest and gave an unhappy sigh.

"I think I would have preferred sleeping in the woods," she mumbled.

"For someone who wants to see the world, you're awfully timid."

She grimaced at him. "Well, did you see the way those men were all staring? It's like they've never seen a woman before."

"Perhaps just not such a beautiful woman," Baris told her. He dropped his pack and went to light the fire. "Why don't you relax? Put away your things and brew us up some tea. I'll fetch something for dinner."

"You're not going out!"

He looked at her as he stood up and brushed the dust from the knees of his breeches. "The door will be bolted. And we're on the second floor. I think you'll be safe enough for a short while. It won't take me long. I promise."

She grabbed his arm. "If you just need to feed, Baris, that's why I'm here."

His stomach flipped at the mere thought of feeding on her again. He desperately wanted to but he wasn't sure if he could trust himself. And he didn't think she needed to be bled quite yet. He could find little iron in her scent.

"That's not why I'm going, Deirdre," he said softly. "I thought I sensed another Vector close by. I want to see if I can pick up any more traces of him. If I can find him, he might be able to help me locate Anika."

"Another Vector? Here? In the middle of nowhere?"

"I am here," he reminded her. "In the middle of nowhere." Gently, he pulled her hand from his arm and kissed it. "I will be very quick. Please, brew up some tea. I'll look forward to having it with dinner. And be sure to bolt the door behind me."

He hurried from the room before she could argue, and glanced about for a back staircase. There didn't appear to be one. With a grimace, he took the main staircase and quietly crept down it until he could see into the main room. The innkeeper was nowhere in sight and Baris hurried to the door and slipped outside. He didn't want anyone to see him go, didn't want anyone to know that Deirdre was there alone. At the same time, he wanted to decrease the amount of time he spent alone with her. Just the thought of bedding down in the same room was already causing a reaction, one that both disgusted and excited him. He put those thoughts and images aside and headed toward an eatery he had noticed upon entering town.

The place was crowded, and hot, various odors mingled in the heavy air like a net to ensnare him. Baris made his way through the crowd and stepped up to the counter. A comely young woman was tending the bar and she gave him a wide, white smile, her gray eyes appraising him unabashedly.

"Kin I get you a drink, sir?" she asked, her voice light and lilting.

"No, thank you, lass," Baris replied. "I want to order some dinner."

"And will ye be eatin' it here? Alone?"

He eyed her with amusement. "No, I'll be taking it back to my room."

"Ye're staying at the inn, then? For a while? Alone?"

Her questions were cloyingly suggestive and Baris gave her a small teasing smile.

"Well, if I told you all of that, then I would have no secrets left, would I? Do you have a menu?"

She smiled back and leaned on the counter, her ample breasts seeming about to tumble from the low-cut bodice of her peasant dress.

"We have soup," she said, her voice almost a purr. "Beef and vegetable. It's served up with hot bread, dripping with butter and sweet--soft--honey. Would ye like to know what we offer for dessert?"

Baris didn't think he needed to ask. Her actions were speaking for themselves. His gaze moved of its own accord to her neck. He could see her pulse there, pounding in anticipation. He took another deep breath and moved his gaze to her eyes.

"Then soup it shall be," he said, keeping his voice cool and detached. "Bread and honey as well. Enough for two, please." He paused a moment, considering her offer, then shook his head. "I won't be needing the dessert but thank you anyway."

She sighed and straightened. "The good ones are always taken," she murmured. She flipped her long, thick golden braid over her shoulder and disappeared into the kitchen to place his order.

Baris chuckled softly then turned slightly to look at those around him. They were a hearty-looking lot, sturdy and muscular. Even the few women were solid-looking. Baris imagined they would have to be to eke out a living in the mountains. He wondered about their livelihood here. There didn't seem to be much in the way of pasture or farmland and he hadn't seen herds of any appreciable size. The surrounding area was mostly forest. He supposed this village could survive on the sale of wood alone, but it would take strong backs to fell the huge trees he'd seen.

"Here ye be," the serving wench said, reappearing with a bundle. "The soup's in covered bowls. Just leave them at the inn. They'll be collected in the morning. If ye'd like to order yer breakfast now, I have a fantastic memory."

"And breakfast consists of more honey?" He couldn't help but tease her.

She giggled. "Eggs and sausage, mostly. But the cook can turn a good-looking flapjack, as well."

He nodded. "Very well. That sounds good. Flapjacks it is, then."

"And yer room number, sir? I can deliver breakfast first thing. Ye won't even have to slip outta yer nightclothes."

Baris couldn't contain his smile as he paid for dinner, throwing in a silver as a tip for the girl. "I'll come pick it up. Good eve."

He noticed her little pout of unhappiness as he turned away with his parcel. He chuckled again and left the eatery. As he walked it occurred to him that even though the young woman had nearly thrown herself at him, he had found no interest whatsoever in her. So, why then, should Deirdre bring out such lustful reactions? It didn't make sense. With a shake of his head, he turned his steps toward the inn. He had almost reached it when a muffled scream cut through the darkness. Startled, he spun toward the sound.

It came from a narrow, dark alley between two sagging buildings. Baris placed his food bundle on the nearest porch and moved quietly in that direction. His exquisite night vision caught movement at once. Two people, a man and a woman, were wrestling at the far end of the alley. Even in the dark, Baris recognized the woman...Deirdre.

He rushed forward, a cry of rage on his lips. The man whirled, abandoning his attack on Deirdre. She stumbled and fell, sobbing, against the wooden walls as Baris stormed up. His hand shot out, his fingers wrapping tightly about her attacker's large throat.

The man gagged and clawed at Baris' arm in panic as the Vector lifted him from the ground. A quick glance showed him that Deirdre's gown was torn almost to her waist.

"How dare you!" he snarled, tightening his grip.

The man kicked and struggled but could not escape Baris' grasp.

"It's--not--what--you--think," he gurgled, his voice barely audible.

"Not what I think? Then pray tell, enlighten me." Baris relaxed his grip just enough that the man could speak coherently.

"She--offered. I--paid--her."

Deirdre gasped with outrage. "That's a lie! I would never offer myself to any man for money!" She once again broke into heaving sobs, covering her face with one hand while futilely trying to hold her dress together with the other.

"No!" the man repeated, his terrified gaze on Baris' face. "I'm not lying! She's a whore!"

Baris clenched his jaw, rage consuming him. "How dare you? I know this woman. And I know her virtues. You have sullied them with your actions and your words." With one quick twist of his wrist, he snapped the man's neck, then flung the lifeless body aside.

Immediately, he turned to Deirdre, gathering her into his arms where she huddled, sobbing and shaking. He smoothed her hair, then pushed her away gently for a moment to pick up her cloak from the ground. He put it around her and pulled it close about her shoulders, then held her again until her crying quieted.

"What were you doing out here?" he whispered.

"Some--someone came to the room," she sobbed. "They were trying to get inside. I got scared. When they left, I came looking for you. Oh, Baris," she gripped his cloak, "do we have to stay here? Can't we just move on? Sleep someplace else? I would be willing to walk the night just to be away from here."

He looked down into her eyes. They were round with fright. Her entire body shook. He hugged her close again. "No, we don't have to stay here," he told her, though his body was crying out for rest. He had spent half the day as a stallion and the fatigue of the shift and the ensuing walk had exhausted him. Still, he would most likely get no sleep in this village anyway. He pulled Deirdre's cloak tighter over her near-nudity and escorted her back down the alleyway to the street.

"I'll have to go back to the inn and fetch our packs," he told her. "And I have a dinner bundle here as well. It's cold by now, I'm sure, but we'll take it with us just the same." He retrieved the parcel from the porch as he spoke and guided Deirdre back toward the inn.

They kept to the shadows; and once they arrived at their destination, Baris drew Deirdre inside. The innkeeper was still nowhere to be found, probably gone off to bed himself. Baris hurried Deirdre up the stairs to their room. Once inside, he quickly bolted the door and grabbed up their belongings.

"Here, change," he instructed her.

She took her pack, then shrugged out of her torn blouse. Baris reluctantly averted his gaze and moved to the window to peer out. He wondered how long it would be before the man's body was discovered. He wanted to be well away from this village before then. It would mean shapeshifting again, however, and Baris wasn't sure how long he could maintain something as large and powerful as a horse.

His thoughts went again to the Vector he thought he had sensed earlier. The traces were gone now and he didn't dare draw on his magic to scan the area. He was probably mistaken anyway. The signs had been so very light...almost not there at all. It was probably just his fatigue playing tricks on him.

"All right," Deirdre said softly. "I'm ready."

Baris turned from the window, involuntarily sucking in his breath. The blouse that Deirdre had chosen to replace her modest torn one was bright yellow and low-cut, barely able to contain her ample breasts. Her unbound dark hair lay against it like serpents coiling about her neck, dipping into her cleavage enticingly, as if beckoning him to follow. He tried to swallow the lust that suddenly threatened to overwhelm him, but his mouth was dry, his throat constricted. At the moment, he didn't much care about the dead man in the alley or the fact that the law might be on its way to his door. All he wanted to do was to follow the tendrils of dark hair and free Deirdre's bosom from its golden cocoon. He watched with dismay as she swept her cloak over her shoulders, covering the creamy mounds.

It was only through sheer force of will that he managed to merely take her hand and lead her from the building. Once in the dark and cold, Baris was able to think more clearly. He noticed the rich scent of iron and turned to Deirdre with the question on his face. "Iron?"

"I tried to stop him," she whispered. "I couldn't. I'm not strong enough."

Baris' fury returned and he gave her hand a gentle squeeze, feeling justified now in having snuffed out the man's life. They slipped through the village and back into the dark forests. Once there, he handed her both packs, then quickly shifted into a horse. She climbed on his back and he took to the trail, flying over the rocky, uneven ground.

He kept up his frantic pace until the first hints of morning played through the skies. He stopped, winded and trembling. He shifted almost before Deirdre could climb from his back. With an exhausted groan, he collapsed onto the sparse field grass. Deirdre dropped down beside him.

"Oh, Baris," she cried, cradling his head in her arms. "You shouldn't have overdone like this. It's my fault. I am so sorry. Please forgive me."

He reached up to pat her arm in reassurance, even as his eyelids fluttered closed. He was simply too tired to keep them open any longer and fell into a deep sleep at once.

He woke late in the afternoon, though the sleep did not seem to have helped much. He still felt weak-limbed and dizzy. Deirdre tended a small fire. She looked over at him with a smile when he finally stirred.

"I've brewed some tea and I've reheated the soup as well. It should help you regain your strength."

Baris struggled to sit up as she poured the amber contents from the teapot to a mug. She handed it to him and he took it with gratitude, breathing deep of the minty aroma. The taste was invigorating, and he let out a sigh of relief.

"Thank you. This will help greatly." He glanced about their surroundings, then up at the sky. "It's almost nightfall. You shouldn't have let me sleep so long."

She laughed. "As if I had a choice. You were dead to the world, Baris. I don't think a thunderstorm could have wakened you."

He grimaced. "Dead to the world? And leaving you unprotected again." He couldn't voice his guilt over leaving her alone at the inn.

She came to sit beside him, handing him a bowl of soup.

"Last night was not your fault," she murmured. "I shouldn't have left the room. I was probably safe there, despite my misgivings. I'm the one who should be blamed."

He shook his head, trying without much success to ignore the view offered by her blouse. He glanced about for her cloak. It was hanging on a low branch, and he both wished it was covering her, and glad that it wasn't. He looked back at her. "No, I should have ordered dinner from the innkeeper. I didn't have to go out."

She gave up the argument and changed the subject. "Did you find that other Vector you thought was in the village?"

"No. I was probably mistaken. The trace was far too slight. It couldn't have been a Vector."

"So, do we continue on towards Nowles?"

"We might as well. I have no other goal. I have no idea where Anika is. Without help from Jaeger and Rhiannon, I may never find her." He sagged as another thought crowded into his already-distraught mind. "She needs to be bled," he said softly. "I know I didn't take enough blood from her before we left home. She could be dying by now."

"She knows how to bleed herself," Deirdre reminded him. "I'm sure she would do so."

"Yes, and then probably be worse off from infection." He finished his tea and soup and struggled to his feet, swaying unsteadily. "We have to go on. Even if Anika no longer wishes to have me as her husband, I still need to find her."

Deirdre began to repack their supplies. Her voice was thoughtful when she spoke. "If you do find Anika and find a cure for whatever you think is wrong with her and she still wants you to leave her, what will you do?"

Baris winced. He didn't know the answer to that. It would surely mean leaving his son. How could he do that? Just walk off, to perhaps never see Thale again?

"I suppose I'll go back to the Lair," he mused. "At least from there I can watch over Thale. I can be with him at a moment's notice but Anika won't have to suffer my presence on a daily basis."

"The Lair? You would live there again? Away from the rest of the world?"

He shrugged. "I suppose so. Without my family, I have nothing here."

Deirdre looked up at him, sadness in her eyes. "But, Baris, why could you not love again? You don't have to be alone."

He gave her a grim smile. "Vectors wait a long time for the right mate to come along. Sometimes it can take hundreds of years. Most of the time it never happens. I was amazingly lucky to have found Anika at this early stage of my life, just after reaching my Growth. It was like a miracle. And when we do find our mate, it's for life, Deirdre. Even if Anika no longer wishes me to be around, she is still, and will always be, my mate. There can be no other."

Deirdre gasped and quickly looked away. Baris frowned, wondering what he had seen in that brief glimpse of her dark eyes. Resignation? Despair? Anger? He shook himself, chasing the questions away, as she spoke, her voice cool and firm.

"I didn't know that. And I don't believe that. I think there is always room in one's heart for further love. I mean, look at children. Would you not love another child? Is all of your love only for Thale?"

"Of course not. But that's a different sort of love."

"And what of your parents? Or your friends? Do you not love them?"

He studied the top of her head. "Again, it is a different type of love. You don't understand."

"Perhaps not," she retorted. "But I still say that the heart is able to love more than once." She finished packing and threw some dirt over the fire, smothering the flames.

Baris sighed and extended a hand to help her to her feet. She took it, her gaze finally meeting his, though she said nothing further about love.

"We'll have to walk, I'm afraid," Baris said. "I am far too drained to shift into anything more substantial than a hawk or a fox. And I don't think you could ride either of those."

His attempt at levity brought only a small smile from Deirdre and the pair set off at a slow pace. For the first time in several days, Baris' thoughts turned to Anika almost exclusively. His worry ate at him. He decided to save his magic and enter the Lair later that night. Even though it would be admitting his failure, he was determined to discuss the situation with Darius. He was sure the Sovereign would be able to find Anika swiftly. Once that was accomplished--well, Baris wasn't sure what he would do. He would check on Thale, make sure that the child was recovering fully from the snakebite. He would see that Anika was bled, her body rid of the excess iron that was no doubt building to toxic levels. And then they would talk. He would tell her how much he loved her, how much he needed her at his side. He would ask her forgiveness for anything he had said or done that might have hurt her. And he would tell her that if she wanted him gone, he would bow to her wishes, although the very thought sent pain ripping through his heart.

He shot a sidelong glance at Deirdre, walking beside him seemingly lost in thought. He would have to see that she was escorted safely back to the village. He felt guilty that he had promised her an adventure, a chance to see the world, yet could not deliver it. He added that disappointment to his growing list of failures.

He pondered her arguments for his finding a second love. Her meaning wasn't lost on him. He was not that naïve...not anymore. He could no longer dismiss the way she looked at him, the way she touched him, as simple friendliness. But he took her infatuation with him as just that. An infatuation. He was a safe haven for her. Someone she could talk to freely, be herself around. He didn't demand anything of her; he wasn't trying to possess her. Baris felt again his anger that Deirdre's father had as good as sold her to Holt. It wasn't right. People shouldn't be traded about like commodities. Baris decided in that moment that he wouldn't take her back to the village if she still didn't want to go. Instead, he would see to it she was set up in a new village, someplace where she could choose her own husband, someone who she loved and who loved her back. He suddenly wanted very badly to help this beautiful young woman as much as she was helping him.

He drew a deep breath, more to savor the fresh scents of the woods about him than to clear his mind. For the first time in days, his thoughts seemed to be on target, focused. Suddenly, the scent of iron assailed his nostrils. He frowned, glancing at Deirdre. She said she had tried to use magic to thwart last night's attack, but this scent was strong...almost too strong for her safety. She would need to be bled, and that thought sent shivers of both anticipation and concern through him.

He was so very aware now of her sensuality, of her desire for him, of his own powerful need to protect her. He sincerely wondered if he could maintain his self-control and integrity once he began to feed on her. He shook his head. Wasn't Anika the one who said maybe he should be with Deirdre instead of with her? Still, the idea brought him as much pain and guilt now as it had when his wife suggested it. He had never considered his friendship with Deirdre might be perceived in any other light. He had been dreadfully wrong, that was clear.

The thought that he had unintentionally hurt his wife sent new waves of despair through him. He had never wanted to do that. Yet, he had apparently done so. Perhaps she was right. Perhaps he didn't deserve her or their son. Perhaps a solitary life in the Lair was what he deserved. A heavy sigh escaped him.

Deirdre looked up at him. "I'm sorry," she said softly.

He turned to her, surprised. "What for?"

"For making you uncomfortable. I know that you love Anika. It just makes me angry that she does not return that love. You deserve more, Baris. You deserve someone who loves you, who will respect you, who will be with you."

He chuckled at the disparity of their thoughts. Here he was thinking that he didn't deserve Anika, while Deirdre had decided that Anika didn't deserve him. It was no wonder that men and women had trouble understanding each other. Their thought processes were so very different when it came to emotions.

"You do not make me uncomfortable, Deirdre," he assured her, if not altogether truthfully. "You are not the cause of Anika's emotional coldness. You have nothing to apologize for."

She pouted. "Well, it's not fair, Baris."

"There are many things in life that are not fair, Deirdre, though I do not consider this one of them." He hesitated before sharing his plans. "I am going to return to the Lair tonight. I will ask Darius to find Anika, bring her to the Lair. I am worried about her condition."

"Will you have enough magic to do that?"

"I think so, if I am careful about using it tonight. I really can't understand my sudden lack of magical prowess. It seems to have hit at a most inopportune time."

"Well, maybe it's just because you're so worried about Anika and Thale. You'll probably get back to normal when all of this is resolved."

"I hope you're right."

They walked the rest of the evening in relative silence, each lost in their own thoughts. If Baris' had been less heavy, he might have actually enjoyed his surroundings. The forest was cool and quiet, with a majestic power he had not felt for a long time. He loved living in the meadows above the raging Callows River but this place of ancient wood called to his spirit. He absently wondered if Anika would enjoy living in a place like this. He wished he could ask her.

Deirdre tugged his sleeve. "Can we stop for a bit?" she asked. "I'm hungry and tired."

Baris glanced up at the sky. Night would be upon them very soon and it was unlikely they would reach Nowles before then. And he had seen absolutely no signs that they were even approaching a village. It appeared they would be sleeping beneath the stars, so there was no sense in pushing Deirdre for no reason. He nodded and dropped the pack, admitting silently to himself that he was feeling just as fatigued as she looked.

"I think I heard water through there," Deirdre said, pointing to a thick cluster of bushes. She unfastened her cloak and laid it aside, though she left her hat on. "I'm going to freshen up and fetch some water for tea. I'll be back in a moment."

"I'll see what I can do about getting a fire started," Baris said. He glanced at the towering trees. "Maybe I can gather enough fir boughs that we can at least make a soft bed for the night." He chuckled at her grimace and handed her the teapot. "Be careful around the river. The rocks can be slippery."

"I'm not a child, Baris," she replied with a slight grimace. She hurried away, obviously intent on a thorough washing in the cold waters.

Baris gathered enough wood for the fire and to last them through the night and had just gotten it into a pile when he heard a splash and a shriek. He dropped the wood he held and dashed toward the sound. The river was bigger and swifter than he'd thought, the water running in white rapids over large boulders and snags. Deirdre had been swept a good distance downriver and now clung to a fallen tree, though the current threatened to rip her away from her anchor.

"Hold on!" Baris cried and scrambled down the muddy bank toward her.

"Hurry!" she screamed, adjusting her position to try for a more secure hold. One arm slipped from the wet wood and she was momentarily pulled under. She resurfaced, gagging and coughing, her dark eyes desperate.

Baris scanned the banks for something he could use to hold out to haul her back to the shore. He picked up a length of branch but it was too short.

"Baris!" Deirdre shrieked again, struggling wildly to retain her hold.

Baris stared at her in bewilderment. Then it came to him. He could shapeshift. A bear would be able to handle the strong current. If he didn't slice Deirdre open with his claws. He set his jaw and called his magic to his aid. It came slowly, grudgingly, and he wondered how long he would be able to maintain the shift. The moment it was complete, he waded into the cold water, finding solid purchase with his large padded feet. It took him only a moment to reach Deirdre. She reached out for him, pure terror in her eyes. Her hand closed about his long, shaggy fur in a desperate grip. He winced at the pain but braced himself against the battering current as she hauled herself onto his back. Once he was sure she was firmly aboard and holding tight, he slogged back to shore.

The shift lasted only long enough for him to climb up the steep bank to solid ground. He collapsed, gasping, and a moment later felt her roll off his back to lie next to him. For a moment, neither of them said a word, being too involved in catching their breath. Then Deirdre broke into sobs.

"I'm sorry," she wailed. "I'm sorry. I should have been more careful. Thank you, Baris. Oh, thank you!" She wrapped her arms about him in a fierce hug, her whole body trembling.

Baris rolled over and held her against his chest, fighting for the strength to stand up. He could feel her shivering.

"Come on. We need to get a fire going. You're soaked. You'll catch your death of chill." He staggered to his feet and helped her up.

"I lost my hat," she sobbed. "My beautiful hat."

Baris stared at her wet and muddy face and suddenly he laughed out loud. "Your hat? That's what you're concerned about? Your hat?"

She looked up at him, dark curls hanging limply on each cheek, water trailing down her neck, disappearing into her cleavage.

"I liked that hat," she mumbled.

The words brought even more laughter. He brushed her wet tangles aside, careful to keep his hands well above that ample bosom that seemed to beckon him to touch.

"I'll get you another, then. Come on." He put one arm about her shoulders and urged her back toward the fire pit.

Once the fire was going, Deirdre huddled near it, shivering uncontrollably, her lips and hands blue. Baris shook his head and pulled his blanket from his pack.

"Get out of those wet clothes," he ordered, handing the blanket to her before yanking his own from where she had stashed it. "Thank goodness you took off your cloak. At least you'll have something to wear until your clothes dry." He held up the second blanket to afford her some privacy, though he could see quite well over the top. He simply didn't have the strength to hold it any higher.

He forced his eyes to lock on the far distance as she peeled off the sodden clothing. Even so, he caught flashes of creamy white skin, filled out in all of the right places. He finally closed his eyes, fighting the temptation that raged through him to throw the blanket to the ground and warm her in a much more pleasant manner. He chastised himself for his thoughts and forced them back to Anika and Thale.

"There," Deirdre announced. "I'm dressed."

He lowered the blanket as she pulled the cloak together in the front.

"Did you lose the teapot as well? Hot tea would help a great deal in warming you up."

"No, I think it's still sitting on the bank."

"I'll fetch it then." He wrapped the blanket about her shoulders and went in search of the teapot. He found it sitting on a flattened muddy spot near the water. As he bent to fill it, his gaze wandered over the area and he frowned. There was really no bank here, just a muddy beach. He didn't see how she could have fallen in. Unless she had waded out to wash and slipped on the stones beneath the water. That was probably it. With a sigh, he stood and returned to the camp. There was no sense in even trying to go to the Lair tonight. Not with the magic he had just expended. He set the teapot near the flames, then turned to unpack something to eat.

Deirdre was still shivering and had huddled into a tight ball, the blanket drawn close. Baris could see water dripping from her hair and he searched for something to dry it with. Not finding anything, he took off his own tunic, then his undershirt. Deirdre looked up at him.

"Too warm?" she teased, her voice trembling.

He grinned and replaced his tunic, shivering as the cool leathers touched his bare skin. "No, but your hair could use some drying. It'll chill you through." He moved around behind her and began to blot the water from her long tresses.

"You didn't have to do that," she protested, albeit not very fiercely. "Now, you'll be too cold."

"I'm fine." And, in truth, he was. Being this close to her was making him very warm. He pushed the desire aside and concentrated on his task, but the more he tried to ignore the lure of her soft skin, the more he wanted it. The scent of iron crashed into his senses, driving his body to react. He needed to feed. He was weak with his last call of magic and Deirdre's overpowering scent was too much for him to resist. He dropped to his knees behind her, stroking her wet hair with gentle wipes of the cloth. The creamy white skin of her neck seemed to glow in the firelight, beckoning him closer and closer. He leaned forward, breathing deep of the intoxicating scent of the iron. A moment later his mouth was on her neck, his arms wrapped about her. She moaned and leaned against him, her breathing sharp and fast. Baris could no longer control himself. He pulled her tight, and fed, not even worrying about the responses his body was experiencing.

Chapter Nine

Baris woke shaky and weak, and yet strangely aroused. He couldn't remember his dreams completely, only that Deirdre had figured prominently in them. He sat up groggily, then shivered as the cold morning air wrapped about him. The fire had gone out. Deirdre was nowhere in sight and Baris staggered to his feet, alarmed. He called her name into the dark woods about him. It seemed to rebound to him, echoing shrilly in his aching head, and he clutched his temples, wincing.

"Baris?"

Her soft voice, concerned and questioning, came from behind him. Baris turned slowly but even so his head spun and he reached out for something to steady himself. He found it in Deirdre's grip.

"What's the matter?" she asked.

"Where were you?" he countered, his tone far more demanding than he had intended. He noticed that she was dressed and was glad of it. The condition he was in, he didn't know if he could resist her if she had been standing even partly nude before him.

"I went to get some more wood," she replied. "I was cold and I used up all we had."

He blinked, only now realizing she held a bundle of branches in the crook of her arm. Guilt at his demanding tone flooded him and he reached for the wood. "Let me."

"No, it's all right. You don't look so well. Maybe you'd better sit down. I'll brew some tea. That should help. And there's still some bread left over from dinner."

He didn't have the energy to argue and collapsed back onto the hard ground, shivering. Deirdre dropped the wood onto the blackened ash, then turned and picked up her discarded blanket. She draped it gently across Baris' shoulders. He gave her a wan smile and pulled the heavy cloth close, pushing aside the urge to pull her inside it with him.

It seemed to take her forever to get the fire started. Forever that he sat and watched her as she bent this way and that, twisting and turning in some strange, exotic dance to entice the wood to flame. At last, smoke wafted into the air, curling upward like a snake slithering into the sky, but no flame appeared. Deirdre leaned over and began to blow softly on the smoldering wood. Again, her bosom threatened to show itself, straining at the thin ties holding it back. Baris stared, fixated, hoping and yet dreading the possibility that those ties would fail. Scowling, he hunched further into his blanket.

He had never been this weak before and could not fathom why he was now. Merely shapeshifting as he had done the night before could not be the reason. He had shifted hundreds of times, into things far more powerful than a bear. Even if he had expended energy in rescuing Deirdre from the river, it still should not be affecting him as it was.

She looked over at him with a shrug of resignation.

"The wood is damp. It seems we will go without tea this morning. Unless, of course, we can find a village. I, for one, would love a decent bed beneath me tonight."

Baris said nothing, forcing his thoughts to Anika. If he was this cold and miserable, what was she enduring? The question plagued him, drove him to his feet, though his knees threatened to drop him back to the hard ground. He had to get to a village, regain his strength and go to the Lair, get help to find his wife. And he needed to see his son, to know that he was all right, that he had recovered from the snakebite.

Deirdre seemed to read his thoughts and hurriedly repacked their meager supplies. She drew her cloak close and came to stand beside him.

"Will you be able to walk?"

He nodded, took the pack and started off, as if in proof. Deirdre stayed close beside him. The idea both irritated and pleased him. It was as if she expected to have to catch his falling body any moment. The thought was almost humorous. If he did topple, there was no way she could support him. She would end up on the ground as well, probably being crushed by his muscular form.

The thought of pressing against her soft curves sent new aching through Baris and he frowned, trying to push the image from his mind. But it remained to torment him and more than once, he glanced at his companion, knowing his lust must show in his eyes. Deirdre seemed not to notice, however, and that only furthered his sense of guilt. Anger at himself drove him forward, his pace fast and long-stepped. Deirdre struggled to · keep up.

At last, she grabbed his arm, stopping him. Her cheeks were flushed from exertion and her chest heaved. Each deep, gasping breath she took threatened to spill her breasts from their fabric cradle. Baris averted his gaze with much difficulty.

"When we get to a village, we need to buy you new clothes," he informed her. "It's too hard to walk in skirts. You need breeches and sturdy boots."

Deirdre frowned. "I don't want to spend any more money. I'm fine."

"No, you're not fine!" he snapped, then was instantly sorry for his tone. "I'm sorry. I didn't mean it that way. I'm just tired and weak. I need to rest."

She gave him a small, understanding smile.

"I know. Why don't I scry for a village? Perhaps if we knew how far away it was, it would help."

Baris hesitated. Though he desperately wanted to know, he wasn't sure about her using magic. He wasn't sure that he could stay away from her once the scent of iron surrounded her again. The thoughts only increased his guilt and once more sent his annoyance with himself rising. He shook his head.

"No, it's too soon for you to use magic. Besides, I don't know that I want you that close to the river again. I'm not up to fishing you out."

Deirdre grinned. "You did make one handsome bear, though."

The words brought a fragile smile to his face. "And you make one beautiful fish."

She laughed and snugged her arm through his. Baris caught at his breath, unsure how her touch would affect him, but to his relief, it brought a warmth only to his skin, not his loins.

It wasn't until late afternoon that they finally saw evidence they were nearing a village. A narrow dirt road emerged from the woods and meandered in a zigzag pattern across a wide field, skirting the rise and fall of the land. Baris and Deirdre climbed one such rise, pausing at the top. A city sprawled out not far away.

"It's big," Deirdre said softly. "I've never been to such a big place before. Even the village where I schooled wasn't this big."

Baris was mesmerized by the wonder and excitement that showed in her eyes. It only increased her beauty and reawakened his desire for her. He gasped when she suddenly turned to him and clutched his cloak with both hands, pulling herself close to him.

"Can we go exploring once we get there? Can we look at all of the finery such a village has to offer?" She looked again toward the city. "I'll bet you can get anything you want in a place like that. So much to see, so much to do. That's the sort of place I want to live, Baris."

"You may change your mind after you get there," he said. "Large villages like this are called cities and they oftentimes have their fair share of troubles."

"What sort of troubles?"

He urged her to walk. "Thieves, mostly. Out to steal whatever they can lay their hands on. Including a woman's virtue. You will have to be careful."

Deirdre's grip on his arm tightened. "I have you to protect me and I won't be stupid enough to go off alone again."

The thought of having to protect her was both inviting and daunting. He still retained images of the man he had killed in the alley. He didn't want a repeat of such. He almost wished they didn't have to go into the city. At the same time, he knew he needed to. He was exhausted and weak. He needed decent food and a place to recover from whatever ailed him. In a few days time, he should be able to go to the Lair. And then, then, he would find Anika.

They reached the outskirts of the city at dusk. Baris quickly shifted into the guise of a middle-aged man, taking his cue from the appearance of the people that crowded the streets, no doubt heading towards supper at one of the various eateries lining the board sidewalks. Horse-drawn carts rumbled past, churning up dust that drifted lazily through the still air, air that was filled with a potpourri of smells. Smoke, roasting meat, fresh-brewed ale, baked goods...all mingled with the scent of dirt, sweat, animal excrement and garbage. It was enough to set Baris' stomach on edge. He grimaced and scanned the streets for a proper inn.

He wanted something nice though not stuffy, comfortable though not costly. Unfortunately, the signs in front gave no hint of what might lay behind the doors and, in the end, he simply chose the nearest.

The lobby was large, well-lit and warm. Baris didn't realize how cold he had been until he was inside. He stepped up to the counter, picked up the small bell and rang it loudly. It took only a moment for the innkeeper to appear. When he did, he wrinkled his nose in obvious disgust at the bedraggled pair before him.

"How may I assist you?" he asked, his voice dripping with disdain.

The tone irritated Baris and he slapped a gold piece, one of his last, onto the smooth wooden counter. He was far too tired to summon the magic that would allow him to retain the room for free.

"A room. With a bath. And two beds."

The man eyed the gold suspiciously, as if doubting its authenticity. Deirdre stepped forward, loosing her cloak at the neck and letting it fall away.

"Please, kind sir," she purred. "We have been through much. Our supplies, but for these small packs, were stolen by vagabonds. We barely escaped with our lives and only then by throwing ourselves into the river. We have spent a cold night in the woods and desperately need a place to recover. My companion is ill as well. Can you help us?"

The man's gaze had locked on Deirdre's bosom and his hard countenance softened. "I see. I understand. The roads can be hazardous at times." He picked up the gold piece, then secured a large, iron key from a pegboard behind him. He handed the key to Deirdre, ignoring Baris completely. "If you need anything else, let me know."

Baris frowned and tapped the counter to regain the man's attention.

"After we freshen up we would like dinner. Can you recommend a place that will have good, hearty food?"

The man started, his gaze snapping back to Baris.

"Yes. Cantor's. It's just over two streets. You can't miss it. Sign's as big as a house."

Baris nodded his thanks and steered Deirdre toward the wide staircase.

"How did you do that?" he demanded in a low voice, though he already had an idea.

"Do what?" Her voice was pure innocence.

"Entrance him so."

She laughed gaily. "I think he simply appreciates the finer points of a woman."

For some reason, the idea of Deirdre using her feminine wiles to get what she wanted grated on his nerves. Some unwanted voice deep inside his head whispered that he was jealous, and he blocked it out. It was ridiculous. He had no right to be jealous. In fact, he should be pleased if she found someone else to turn her attentions on.

"Here's the room," she said, stopping before a six-paneled wooden door. She fit the key in the lock and opened it.

The place was more than comfortable. It was almost luxurious. Baris wondered just how many nights the gold piece had bought in such an extravagant place. He dropped the packs on the floor and closed the door. Deirdre had already gone into the next room to inspect the bath. She returned, dropping her cloak on the nearest chair, a smile on her face.

"The bath is huge," she declared. "We could both fit in there at the same time."

Baris' gaze darted to her in surprise. "Both?"

She gave him a teasing grin. "I just meant it was big. Although--" She let the sentence trail off as she looked at him from half-closed eyes.

Baris shook his head, though his body was already saying yes.

"You go on ahead. I want to rest for a bit." He dropped into a chair hearthside, dredging up just enough magic to set the wood laid in it ablaze.

Deirdre giggled and came up behind him to knead his shoulders. "You're too tense, Baris. You need to relax."

"If I were in the bath with you, Deirdre, relaxation would be the farthest thing from my mind," he mumbled, closing his eyes under her gentle touch. "Go on. Please."

He started when he felt her soft lips against his neck and opened his eyes to look up at her as she pulled back. She smiled at him, ran one finger along his cheek, then slipped away. He watched the bathroom door close, his heart racing. By the Sovereign, how he wanted to follow her!

He surged from his chair, anger at his own weakness overwhelming him, and stomped to the window to peer into the dusty streets.

"Anika," he whispered, feeling like a traitor for even daring to say her name. Tears came unbidden, a result of his fatigue, guilt and grief. He sagged against the wall, lifting his gaze to the dark skies. "Anika, I'm so sorry. I drove you away. You know me better than I know myself. Please, Anika, forgive me."

Chapter Ten

He felt much better and much more in control after a long, hot bath and a good meal at Cantor's. He had taken Deirdre shopping before dinner and though he had purchased her a set of good sturdy traveling leathers, she pleaded for a new dress to wear to dinner. She put her hair up in a gleaming coronet atop her head and even dusted a little powder on her wind-burned face. She looked radiant and Baris noticed many heads turning to watch her as she walked past. Despite his rioting emotions, it felt good to have such a lovely woman on his arm.

Now they strolled the sidewalk beneath the light of a full moon and well-placed lanterns. A gentle breeze blew against them, bringing the fresh scent of water. Baris had inquired and been told that there was a large lake just east of town within easy walking distance. It was where he and Deirdre were headed.

The shoreline had been seeded with grass and planted with wildflowers, giving it a park-like setting. Lamps were placed around the entire circumference of the lake, their light glowing on stone benches set at intervals about the body of water. The benches were close enough together to ensure safety but far enough apart to ensure privacy. Baris led Deirdre to one such bench, noticing that lovers inhabited those on either side.

"Oh, Baris," Deirdre sighed. "This is so beautiful."

"Yes, it is," he agreed, though his gaze was more on her than on the scenery. He watched the wind ruffle stray tendrils that had escaped her hair clips, then forced himself to look away. "So, this is the type of place you yearn to live in?"

"Yes! It's wonderful here! Did you see the sign on the theater? They have plays here, actual plays, performed by actors. I've heard about them but I never dreamed I would be in a place that actually had them."

"Would you like to see a play while we're here?"

She turned to him with a whimper of delight. "Oh, yes! I would love to. But...the clothes, the room, the dinner...you've already done too much, Baris. I can't ask more of you."

He shushed her with a finger to her lips. "I want to, Deirdre. If you are going to experience life in other parts of the country, then you need to experience it all. You can't do that traipsing about in the woods. We'll stay here a few days while I recover, and take in the sights."

She looked away, her face in shadow so that he couldn't see it. "Will you try to return to the Lair again?"

"Yes, when I feel better."

"Will you--will you stay there?"

"Not just yet," he assured her. "I'll have Darius find Anika. Once I make sure she is all right and that Thale is all right, then I will have to make a decision on what to do with my life. Take my word, though, Deirdre, I will not leave you in this town unless and until you are comfortable here."

She cocked her head at him, showing him her full mouth quirked wryly. "You mean, until I find a man to wed, someone to take care of me."

He laughed to cover the sudden pang the words gave him. He didn't want another man to take care of her. He wanted to do it.

"No, I meant until you had a way to support yourself and a sure place to live. I don't want to leave you in the streets."

"With what happened in that last village, I definitely don't want to be in the streets." She shivered and pressed closer to him. He draped his arm about her shoulders protectively. They sat in silence for a while, gazing at the moonlight sparkling on the lake. Baris could hear the whispered proclamations of love from the other couples. He could hear their wet, passionate kisses and their soft moans of desire. It was doing nothing to squelch his own. He didn't have the slightest idea how he was going to get through the night in the same room as Deirdre. The sensible thing would be to procure another. Yet, he knew that Deirdre would not want that. She was still upset over being left alone before. He didn't want to upset her further.

"We should be getting back, I suppose," he said softly, standing up and pulling her with him. "It's getting chilly out here."

"But it's so beautiful," she protested with a resigned sigh. "Can we come back, Baris? Maybe tomorrow night?"

He smiled. "I thought you wanted to see a play."

"I do," she admitted, as they began the walk back toward town. "And I want to stroll the shops, as well, and maybe go to that huge bookshop I saw, and visit the silversmith. And...oh, Baris! Look!" She stopped short, pointing into the darkness. Baris followed her gesture. A huge, stately home sat back from the road, its lush gardens bordering the lake. Candlelamps hung from trees, shedding a yellow glow over the well-kept grounds. Men and women dressed in finery strolled about or chatted in small groups. Laughter and conversation drifted on the night breeze.

"Oh, Baris," Deirdre whispered, "It's a social party."

"A what?"

"A social party. Only the richest and finest people in a town are invited. Oh, how I wish I could attend such a gathering. Come on, let's sneak closer."

She took his hand and pulled him off the road and into the brush. He followed reluctantly, wondering how she knew about such things and yet beginning to share her sense of excitement. They stopped at the perimeter of the gardens. They were close enough to hear the water splashing in the fountains, to hear the clink of fine crystal as glasses were brought together in frequent toasts. Baris could even smell the costly liqueur that seemed to be flowing freely amongst the honored guests in attendance. He glanced down at Deirdre and caught his breath.

He had never seen her looking so radiantly lovely. The moonlight shone in her dark eyes, alight with their own inner glow. The lamplight caught her hair, putting a golden halo about her head. Her smile was dreamy, her face flushed with pleasure as she gazed upon those before her.

And suddenly Baris wanted her to be a part of it. He wanted to see her strolling and mingling with the elite, the high society. He wanted to hear her laughter mixed in with that of the people at the party. He wanted her to be accepted, welcomed, included. He gripped her hand and pulled her past the hedge and into the gardens. She gasped, hanging back.

"What are you doing?" she whispered, panic in her eyes.

"Mingling," he whispered back and drew her straight into the crowd.

No one even seemed to notice. Baris picked up two glasses off the tray of a passing servant and handed one to Deirdre. She took it with a shaky hand.

"Just act like we've always been here," he instructed. "No one will know any different."

"Baris, we'll be arrested. We have to get out of here." Her voice was husky with a combination of excitement and fear.

"We'll be fine. Just smile that lovely smile and walk with me." He moved away, Deirdre close to his side.

Several of the other guests nodded a greeting as they passed but no one stopped them to question who they were. They entered the manor house easily.

Inside, the elegance continued. The hall was huge, the walls covered with finely woven tapestries. Velvet-covered chairs lined the walls, while the center of the floor had been cleared for dancing. Indeed, there were numerous couples already enjoying the music of a small orchestra playing in one corner. Baris set his glass down and offered his hand to Deirdre. She flushed, laughed, and accepted. He placed her glass next to his and led her to the dance floor. At first she was stiff and awkward but once she realized that no one was going to burst through the door to seize them and throw them out, she melted into his arms.

Baris held her close, savoring the silky softness of her hair, the light scent of the perfume she wore, the pressure of her body against his. A tap on his shoulder startled him and he looked into the face of a young man.

"Might I interrupt this dance?" the man asked, his gaze on Deirdre.

Baris started to protest, not willing to let her go. Then, he remembered his Illusion was that of a man old enough to be Deirdre's father. No doubt that's what the young man thought as well. Baris smiled and placed Deirdre's hand into the other man's waiting palm.

"You may indeed," he said, noticing a slight hint of something...fear?...creep into Deirdre's eyes. "I will be close."

"No fear," the man said. "I will be the ultimate gentleman with such a vision of loveliness."

Deirdre blushed and Baris slipped away. He watched as Deirdre and the young man swirled away, moving gracefully through the other dancers. He knew he should be happy for her. This was what she wanted. A place in society, with the elite. Surely this young man was of money. And he was clearly interested in Deirdre. Yet, every fiber of Baris' being prickled with jealousy. He despised the easy way the young man held Deirdre, the closeness. And he tightened his jaw when he saw the man plant a gentle kiss on Deirdre's cheek. He barely noticed that someone had moved in beside him.

"Friend Vector," the man said quietly, in their own tongue. "Greetings."

Baris whirled, surprised. He nearly choked on his gasp, and quickly bowed. "Greetings, Elder," he managed.

The man chuckled. "Your mind is clearly pre-occupied that you didn't sense my presence. At the least, you are aware enough to know my rank. My name is Quentin." He gestured toward Deirdre. "She is quite lovely. A witch?"

Baris hesitated. He knew full well of the lust Vectors held for a witch and a bleeder. He was glad that Deirdre had not used her magic recently. There was no scent of iron to give her bleeder status away. Quentin laughed again and clapped Baris on the shoulder.

"Don't worry," he said. "I have no designs on your mate. Though I must admit I envy you."

"She's not my mate, Elder," Baris replied hastily, then wished he'd said nothing.

"Oh?"

"She...she is my--traveling companion."

The knowing smile with which Quentin responded said exactly how he had interpreted that.

"You are both unfamiliar to me. Tell me, how did you get into the party? I would have known had you been on the guest list."

Baris felt the color creep toward his cheeks. "We...we rather dropped in."

"Oh? How incredibly brash." He laughed, which somehow didn't make Baris feel any more comfortable. In fact, the words irritated him. Still, he knew better than to show that irritation to an Elder, and so calmed his voice when he spoke.

"We are only in town for a few days. We happened to be passing by on our way back from the lake and she told me she had always wished to attend a party such as this. I obviously don't have time to establish myself as one of the elite, but, as you can see, she fits in quite well, despite having no invitation." He changed the subject. "Perhaps you can do me a favor. I am searching for another witch, a male. He is traveling with a Vector. Might you have seen them pass this way?"

"No, I can't say as I have. However, I did hear a man was killed in a village not far from here. His neck was snapped, apparently without a struggle. It would take a very powerful man to do that. Perhaps even a Vector."

Baris' stomach churned uneasily. "That was my doing, Elder," he admitted. "But it was not without provocation. He attacked my companion."

"Just the same, it brought attention to our kind. I, personally, don't like that kind of attention. It has taken me a long time to reach the position I have here. I don't like having that position threatened, particularly by strangers. I suggest you and your companion move on in the morning."

Baris drew himself up in annoyance, trying to keep his tone civil. "We were planning to stay for a few days. I am only just recovering from an illness. And my companion needs time out of the damp and cold of the forests."

"An illness?" He snorted. "Witchery, you mean."

"Witchery?"

"You reek of her magic, my friend. Perhaps she has you under more of a Spell than you can even guess, eh?" He drained his glass and set it on a nearby table. "In the morning, you will leave. Is that clear?"

"And you are who to enforce this?"

Quentin stiffened, one eyebrow arching in annoyance. "Besides being an Elder, I am your savior. It is well known that your companion was the last person seen with the deceased. It should take little imagination to place you as the murderer. In fact, morning might be too late. Think on my words." He turned and strode away.

Baris stared after him in shock. His words made little sense. Witchery? A spell? Baris shook his head, wondering whatever had possessed him to speak to a Lair Elder the way he had, and went after Deirdre. She seemed eager to be relieved of her dance partner, though he did not seem to share the same feeling. He held to her hand.

"We are not done dancing," he informed Baris, his voice cool and aloof.

"We must be going," Baris returned, making an effort to remain polite. "It is late and we have an early morning."

"Another hour at the most," the young man insisted. "I will take her home."

Baris frowned. "No, thank you. She will come now."

The man pulled Deirdre aside, placing himself between her and Baris. "That is her choice, not yours."

Baris took a deep breath to calm himself and looked past the man to Deirdre. She slipped her hand free and attempted to step around. Her demanding partner blocked her. Anger flitted through Baris and he gripped the man's upper arm in a tight hold, physically moving him aside as if he were no more than a child. He saw surprise flash across the man's face.

"Come, Deirdre," Baris said firmly. "We are leaving." He took her hand and turned away.

"Baris!"

Deirdre's cry of warning was shrill, panicked. Baris whirled, catching a glint of silver as the young man whipped a long, shiny dagger from his belt sheath. Several women nearby screamed and scrambled out of the way. Two fainted and were nearly dragged from the dance floor by their panicked partners. The young man drove forward, the dagger uplifted, anger and determination on his lean face. Baris caught his arm, stopping the dagger's downward path in mid-flight. Pure rage tore through him as he bent the man's arm back, his grip growing tighter and tighter. He heard the bone snap, and his would-be assassin shrieked in agony, going white, then limp. The dagger clattered to the floor.

"Enough!" Quentin drew alongside, his face tight with fury. "Leave! Now!" he commanded Baris.

Baris released his hold on the young man, who sagged to the floor, barely conscious, then turned on Quentin, astonishing himself once again at his venom-filled words. "I suggest you check your guest list a little more thoroughly next time. If I could arrive unannounced, it's obvious anyone could. Even scum like him." He gripped Deirdre's arm and pulled her after him.

They left the house through the front. Baris didn't slow his pace until they were well down the street from the estate. It was only then that he realized he was going in the opposite direction of the inn. He stopped, his breathing hard and fast, his jaw tight with anger. Deirdre looked up at him, then suddenly she began to chuckle. He stared at her in confusion.

"Oh, Baris," she managed through her laughter. "I guess I'm just not high society at all. What a mess I made of things. We will be the talk of the town on the morrow. And it's not the kind of talk I was hoping for. I guess this city is not one that I can hope to put down roots in."

"It is hardly your fault, Deirdre. I was the one who took you in there. I was the one who allowed that pathetic excuse of a man to dance with you. And I was the one who used my strength against him."

"Yes, to rescue me. Again. My brave knight." She rose on tiptoe to kiss his cheek.

He was at once assailed with the scent of iron and stared at her, his curiosity evident. She nodded.

"I pulled my magic. I thought I might need to use it. But you handled things very well."

He thought back to the other Vector's words. "Deirdre, have you--did you--?"

"Did I what?"

He looked into her eyes, saw the innocence there and shook his head. "Nothing. Never mind. Let's go back to the inn. I want to leave tomorrow."

"Tomorrow! But I thought we were going to go to the play tomorrow night!"

"We cannot. We need to move on." He couldn't stand the look of disappointment in her eyes and he kissed her cheek gently. "I promise you, the next town we enter, we will take in a play. But we cannot stay here."

She sighed but nodded and linked her arm through his. "All right. But remember, you promised."

He grimaced, hoping he could keep that promise, and led her back toward the inn. He wasn't quite sure how to tell her that they were being sought for murder.

They left just after daylight the next morning. Even so, the streets were crowded and the gossip rampant. Deirdre walked beside him, head held high, though her cheeks flamed at the murmurings of the crowd around her. Apparently, the story of the previous night's encounter...and their descriptions...had already made the rounds. Baris went directly to the nearest livery stables, intending to buy horses, but the stablemaster refused him a sale, stating that the boy he had injured had been the son of a good client. Baris was in no mood to argue the point.

"Pity," he said coldly. "I was prepared to give you twice what they were worth."

Disappointment flashed across the stablemaster's face but Baris turned away. His steps were fast and furious, and he near-dragged Deirdre along the sidewalk and out of town.

"I feel like every eye in that town is on me," Deirdre whispered. "Like there's a target drawn on my back."

Baris frowned but said nothing. He stepped from the road and drew her into the cool confines of the woods, away from the stares. For a while they walked in silence, then Baris stopped and turned to face her. He had to know.

"I must ask this," he said softly. "It is something that was brought to my attention by our host at the party."

"He was another Vector, wasn't he?"

Baris nodded, surprised that she had seen through Quentin's Illusion. "He was. He told me that I reeked of your magic. That I had been Spelled."

Deirdre sighed, averting her gaze. He placed one long finger beneath her chin and forced her to look at him.

"Is this true? Have you been using your magic on me?"

She dropped her gaze. "Yes." Her answer was barely audible.

"Why? For what purpose?"

"Oh, Baris." She reached up and grasped his hand in hers. "You've been so despondent over Anika and Thale. I only wanted to ease some of your suffering. I thought maybe if you could just rest, just relax, you would feel better."

"Rest? Relax?"

She nodded. "Yes. Chamomile tea does that. It's for soothing the mind and body. Peppermint just gives some added strength."

"And that's all? Tea for soothing and strengthening?"

She looked up at him, puzzled. "Yes. Well, maybe a little healing magic in both areas. But, Baris, you were so tired and so depressed. I just wanted to make you happy. You have been feeling better, haven't you?"

For a moment he merely studied her. He couldn't deny that her magic had helped his emotions. Perhaps too well. He had almost hoped that all of his desires, his lust for her, his immoral thoughts were the result of her magic. Guilt was again his companion. How could he have considered trying to blame her for his own failings? How could he shift the responsibility for his dishonorable actions onto her? He shook his head and drew her close.

"Yes, Deirdre," he admitted. "I have been feeling better. " He kissed the top of her head and released her. "We need to keep moving. Hopefully, we can find a smaller village to stay tonight." He started away.

"Baris." She clutched his arm and stopped him. "What's wrong? You seem...I don't know...worried."

He shot her a glance then continued walking.

"I am. I am worried about what may have befallen Anika. I am worried about the injury my son sustained. I am worried about the fact that my magic seems to have left me."

"No, I know all of that. There's something else."

He paused, then sighed. "We are being sought, Deirdre, for the murder of the man in the alley."

"What! Why? He's the one who attacked me! What was I supposed to do? Let him?"

"No." Baris took hold of her arms, noticing that she was trembling. "No, he was in the wrong. I suppose what we should have done was to stay in the village and speak our side. Now the townspeople have only bits and pieces of information. And they are definitely not in our best interest."

"What are we going to do?" she whispered, stepping in closer to lean against his chest, her arms clinging to his waist.

"For now, nothing. I must get to Jaeger. I must find Anika. After I am sure that my wife and child are well and cared for, then I will return to the village to face trial."

"No! You can't! It wasn't your fault! They'll just lock you away, or--or--

No!" She burst into tears.

Baris soothed her, resting his cheek against the softness of her hair. "I will speak the truth, Deirdre, that's all I can do. I cannot run forever."

"Then I'll come as well! It was because of me that it happened in the first place."

Baris was touched at the offer but shook his head. "Just because your clan has accepted the Vectors doesn't mean that other people have. We are still feared by many, despised by most. They would simply assume that you are under my spell and lying to defend me, and they would condemn you as well."

"Well, if you think you're going back there to face their wrath alone, then think again!"

Baris almost laughed at the haughty tone. "Deirdre, sweet Deirdre, you are a most special young woman. For now, let's not dwell on it. Let's just concentrate on finding a place to stay tonight. Perhaps we can even seek news of Vail."

She reluctantly nodded agreement. "Remember? I told him to meet us in Nowles. He's probably on his way there now."

"And we should have been there by now as well," Baris said. "It is obvious I have taken the wrong road." He thought on his own words, wondering why that had not crossed his mind until now. He shook the confusion away. "In the next village we will have to ask directions."

"Do men do that?" Deirdre teased, her indignation vanished as quickly as it had come.

Baris couldn't help but smile. "Yes, but we don't often admit to it." He took her hand and once more began to walk. It was sometime later before either of them spoke and then it was only because the thought would not leave Baris alone.

"Holt said he would come looking for you in a week's time. It's been nearly that."

Deirdre grimaced. "Has it?"

Baris glanced at her. "Will he come looking? Is his possessiveness that strong?"

She was quiet a moment. "I don't know. I think it is. But he won't find me. I won't let him."

"How will you stop him?"

"I don't know. I just will. I will not go back to the village and become a wife to that man. I just won't. I would rather go back to that town and have everyone think I am a low-bred."

Baris lifted his eyebrows in amusement. "You are not a low-bred, Deirdre. You fit in quite well at that party, with those people. It was me who did not fit."

"Not true, Baris. I saw many of the women watching you. You could have had your pick of them all."

Baris cringed, thinking of Anika. Was that what she thought as well? That he could have his pick? That he was casting his gaze elsewhere?

There was no question his recent actions and thoughts of Deirdre had been immoral. It definitely wasn't the way a happily married man should be thinking. His mind should have been on Anika, not on Deirdre's luscious bosom. So why did it seem so often lately that Anika was only a passing thought? He had left his village consumed with the need to heal her, to bring her back to him, emotionally and physically. Now he was traipsing about the woods with a lovely young woman that he dreamed of bedding.

Quentin's words came back to haunt him. Witchery? Was there more to it than what Deirdre claimed? After all, he could feel her desire for him. He was not in this alone. Was she using her magic to lure him? To taunt him? To steal him from his true love?

No. He shook the thought aside, almost laughing at the stupidity of it.

Why would she? What could she gain by it? She knew he loved Anika. She knew he could never find another mate. Here he was again, forcing his own emotions onto her, making it seem that she desired him as much as he desired her. Perhaps he thought it would ease his tremendous guilt if that were the case.

Still, he decided that maybe he had better stop drinking her special teas. Perhaps they were promoting far too much "rest and relaxation" on his part. He needed to be more in control, better able to handle his seemingly adolescent emotions. Although he wasn't quite sure how he could tell Deirdre that.

The rest of the morning was spent trying to find an easy route back to a respectable road. While Baris was sure they were now moving in the right direction... toward Nowles...he wasn't sure how he had become so disoriented. And he was feeling a bit stronger as well. Maybe even that small amount of rest he had managed in the last town had helped. Still, he knew what he really needed was blood. He wondered if Deirdre would be too upset if he sought it elsewhere. With the way his emotions were running, he wasn't sure he wanted to be that intimate with her again.

He suppressed a soft groan. Why couldn't he separate his desires from his needs? Even someone this new to his full Growth should have more control than this. Again, Quentin's words pounded through his head. And, again, he forced them aside. Deirdre had explained it and that was that.

"Look!" She pointed ahead then turned to beckon Baris closer.

He had dropped back as they walked and now hurried to reach her side. What he saw sent confusion raging through him. A huge city sprawled out on the valley floor, the river cutting it in two. Numerous bridges crossed the expanse of water, connecting what appeared to be a business district with a more industrial area. Baris stared at it.

"What? I thought we were going toward Nowles." He looked behind him, then up at the sky, as if they could explain his disorientation. "That certainly isn't Nowles. And I think I would have remembered such a large city anywhere near Nowles. Where the hell are we?"

"Well," Deirdre said. "Why don't we go into the city and find out? You said you would ask for directions. I want to see if you really will."

Her gentle teasing could not rouse a smile and she frowned, linking her arm through his and pulling him along the trail. He followed obediently, still trying to make some sense of his whereabouts.

The trail soon widened, then merged with a narrow lane. It wasn't long before that widened more and became a true road leading through scattered groups of houses into the city proper. Baris took a moment to Illusion himself as a young man to discourage anyone who might want to do more than admire the woman with him. He tightened his grip on Deirdre's hand and led her along the crowded streets.

The mood of the citizens seemed to be jovial. They rushed back and forth across the street, dodging wagons and carts. Their voices were raised in an excited pitch, and Baris was very conscious of how many young people were milling about. Youths and children of all ages giggled and played on the wide, wooden sidewalks and on the small, green, patches of grass between buildings.

There was an extremely festive mood about the entire place.

Deirdre pulled him to a stop in front of a mercantile. She placed one finger on a tattered bit of parchment nailed to the wood.

"A festival," she said, her voice soft and filled with wonder. "There's a festival going on." She spun on him, her dark eyes alight with childlike excitement. "Can we go, Baris? Oh, please, say yes. Please, please."

He regarded her with surprise, then smiled. "To the festival? Why would you want to go there? It's probably just crowded with minstrels, thespians, jugglers, strange and exotic animals..."

"Oh!" she interrupted. "Please!"

He could not contain his laughter. "You've convinced me. But first, we need to find a place to stay the night and a place to get decent food. I am not about to spend my money on the vile offerings at a festival."

She nodded and skipped along beside him, her excitement barely contained. It didn't take them long to secure a room and get directions to a nice pub. Baris had wanted her to remain in her traveling leathers but Deirdre insisted on wearing her gown. She brushed her hair until it shone, then clipped it up away from her face. She positively glowed as the two of them took to the streets.

Baris glanced sideways at her, then tucked her arm under his. She was beautiful and she was on his arm. His. He didn't see how things could get any better.

Chapter Twelve

They returned to the inn very late that night. Dinner had been exquisite, filling Baris' senses with tastes, smells and textures. Succulent roast lamb; small new potatoes; steamed baby carrots swimming in fresh butter; soft hot bread and a thick warm custard dripped with caramel for dessert. All washed down with a spicy white wine that set Baris' tongue tingling and his mood soaring. He couldn't remember when he had last experienced such a wonderful dining experience.

After dinner, he and Deirdre strolled the festival grounds for hours, taking in every sight, performance and play they could. He bought her a sugary confection, then laughed when it stuck to her hair and nose. He kissed it away with no thought as to what he was doing. For the first time in months, he was happy, relaxed and completely at peace with himself despite the fact that he had paid for everything with only his Vector magic. Magic that suddenly seemed easy to gain.

"Oh, Baris! That was wonderful!" Deirdre exclaimed as he closed the room's door. She flopped onto the large, opulent bed with a contented sigh.

Baris chuckled. "So, I take it that you are enjoying at least some of your look at the world beyond your village?"

"Oh, yes! This is more wonderful than anything I could have imagined, Baris." She leapt off the bed and danced across the room to embrace him. "And I have you to thank for it. Thank you, Baris, thank you so much."

He held her close, breathing deeply of the perfume that caressed him as gently as the air itself. "You're very welcome. But I suppose that any thought of returning home is a thing of the past?"

She paused then drew away from him. Slowly, she unclipped her hair, letting it tumble over her shoulders and back.

"I don't know. I mean, this has all been so exciting, so different and wonderful. Still, there's a lot to be said for the quiet life in the woods." She tossed him a seductive glance.

He raised his eyebrows, understanding quite well what she meant. Still, he wished to tease her further. "Then you miss home? You're having second thoughts about returning to Holt?"

"No!" She stared at him in horror. "Not about Holt. I will not...*not*...marry that man! And if returning home means that I must, well, then, I won't go home. I'll find a place here or maybe with that traveling show. I could really see the world then."

He laughed. "And you would do what with the traveling show? You're not an acrobat, you're not an animal trainer. I suppose you could get yourself a crystal ball and read fortunes."

She tossed him a sour look. "A fortune teller? I can't even tell my own future. How could I tell others?"

"Well, from what I have witnessed, all you have to do is make something up. Tell people what they want to hear. Make them happy."

"That's cheating," she said, moving toward the fireplace. She swung the crank over the hot coals then poked at them to encourage a flame.

Baris watched, uneasy for the first time that night. "Why don't we forego the tea tonight, Deirdre? I'm exhausted. And besides, there are other things that I need more than tea."

She looked over at him, a warm smile on her lips. "I thought you would never ask. I've been needing it as well."

As usual, Baris was unsure just how to approach the situation. He frowned, glancing first at the bed then at the divan before the fire. "Perhaps it would be best if we sat there."

She removed her cloak then settled on the lounge. Baris hung his own cloak on the peg by the door then started toward her slowly. He was annoyed with himself for his awkwardness. He felt like a schoolboy about to receive his first kiss. Deirdre looked up at him, smiling mysteriously.

"How did you ever survive all of these years when you find feeding so embarrassing?"

"It's not that I find it embarrassing, Deirdre. Until I met Anika, I rarely knew my source personally. Then when I met and married her, familiarity made it easy. Plus, there's the fact that before I married, I had not yet--" He paused, blushing, unsure if he wished to discuss the details of his Growth with Deirdre.

She placed one hand on his arm. "I know about the Growth, Baris," she said, her voice husky. "I know how it affects the feeding. It's nothing to be ashamed about. It's a physical reaction that you have no control over."

Baris studied her a moment, wondering if that was entirely true. If he really put his mind to it, couldn't he squelch his body's reaction? Or was it because he simply didn't want to? He reached out and touched the ends of her hair, rubbing the silken strands between his fingers. She was breathtakingly beautiful tonight, more so than he had ever seen her. He wasn't sure if it was the firelight dancing off her dark hair or the residual excitement that glowed in her eyes or just his mounting sexual tension. She leaned toward him and their lips met in a gentle, yet passionate, kiss. Her hands slid to the base of his neck, pulling him closer. He responded by tangling his hand in her hair, as his tongue met hers in a dance of desire.

His free hand moved up her side, felt the soft roundness of her breast. Deirdre let out a soft moan, her own desires clearly evident. She leaned backward and he fell atop her on the lounge. All reason left him. He wanted her, entirely. Now! His hands moved over her body, as his breath quickened. Deirdre easily stripped him of his tunic then ran her fingers lightly along his back and sides. The touch sent shivers racing through him and he abruptly stood, drawing her with him. It didn't take but a moment for her to shed her gown. Baris picked her up and placed her gently on the bed then lay beside her, again claiming her lips with his.

The scent of iron wafted into the air, calling out to his Vector need. He moved his mouth to her neck, where he kissed and teased, before finally biting. Deirdre shuddered beneath him.

Her deft fingers easily loosened his breeches, slipped them away from him. She touched him, her soft, warm hands sending waves of lust roaring through him. He slowed his draw of blood, wanting to make it last, wanting to ride to orgasm with her. When she abruptly lifted her legs and wrapped them about his waist, driving him ever deeper into her softness, he could no longer stand the tension. He allowed the blood to flow into his mouth as easily as his seed flowed into her body.

She let out a scream of pleasure, holding to him, moving with him. Then, satiated, he collapsed against her, his mouth still at her neck though he no longer fed. Her warm breath touched gently at his throat, sending a quiet calm through him. He didn't want to move, didn't want to think about any other moment than the one he was in.

Slowly, very slowly, he spiraled down from his euphoria. Guilt began to creep in, though it came on kitten's feet, softly, barely noticeable. He wondered about that as he gently pulled away. She lay still, eyes closed, her breathing returning to normal, her swollen lips curved in a smile of utter satisfaction. Baris brushed dark curls from her face and shoulders, then gently kissed her breasts, throat and lips. She sighed and nestled closer to his warmth. He pulled the blankets over their nude bodies and closed his eyes to sleep.

He woke muzzy-headed and fatigued. Deirdre was snuggled up against him, still asleep. If guilt had come on kitten's feet the previous night, it now came roaring forward with the force of a lion. Baris let out a heavy sigh of disbelief and stumbled from the bed, waking Deirdre in the process.

"What's wrong?" she murmured, peering up at him.

"Nothing. I...it's just time we were up."

"To do what? Can't we just stay here for a few days, Baris? We can keep a low profile, just go out at night. This city is so exciting. We haven't even begun to explore all it has to offer."

Baris picked up the robe supplied by the inn and slipped it on before moving to the window to peer out. The streets were already busy and his gaze flicked over the crowd. A dark-haired woman caught his eye and he stared at her for a long time. She reminded him of Anika, his wife, his lover, his soulmate. How could he have done this to her? How could he have forsaken his vows of fidelity like this?

Anger tore through him and he spun from the window, searching for his clothes. Deirdre watched him dress in silence, her unspoken question hanging in the chill air. When he headed for the door, however, she bolted from the bed and blocked his path.

"Where are you going?" she demanded.

"Just out, Deirdre. I just have to go out." He refused to look at her nudity.

"If this is because of what happened last night..."

"Of course, it's because of what happened last night!" he shouted. "It was wrong, Deirdre! I'm a married man. I love my wife. And now I've done the one thing that is sure to put an end to my marriage and my family. I am below contempt." He pushed past her.

"Baris! Please, don't go."

He paused a moment with his hand on the latch, then shook his head and left the room. His steps were fast and furious, taking him along the wide corridor, down the spiraling staircase and out the front door of the inn. Early morning sunshine hit him full in the face, nearly blinding him. Frowning, he slipped into the shadows created by the tall buildings.

He swung into an alley, barely conscious of the filth that lay on the ground. From alley to alley he went, heedless of his direction, uncertain of his goal. He just wanted to get away. Away! He stopped suddenly. Away from what? From Deirdre? From the inn? From the memory of what had taken place there?

By the Sovereign! Just walking away couldn't erase the fact that he had made love with another woman. And that he had enjoyed it. By the gods, how he had enjoyed it! Even now, the memories were enough to tease his body, to taunt him. He roared out an epithet and once more began walking. Several times he saw men passed out from drink, empty or half-empty bottles clutched in their cold hands. Baris plucked up one such bottle and took a long swallow of the bitter ale. It burned a path to his stomach and he took another, subconsciously realizing he was punishing himself. That only made his anger stronger and he drained the bottle of its contents. With a disgusted oath, he hurled it against a building, watching it shatter. The drunk grunted and shifted position.

Baris glared down at him, at his neck, now exposed. He started toward the man, then stopped. No, not a drunk. He wanted someone else, someone he could command and control, lure with his power. His anger driven to fury by the drink on an empty stomach, he strode onward. If he was destined to be a Lair Vector, living out his life in relative solitude, away from a one-on-one relationship then so be it. He needed to get used to using his power and accept that there would always be a sexual component to it.

He rounded a corner, nearly colliding with a young man coming the other direction. The youth glared up at him, his eyes barely focused.

"Watch where you're going!" he snarled and made as if to push Baris aside.

Baris stood his ground, his hands closing into fists at his side.

"Perhaps you should be the one watching," he said tightly.

The young man started to speak, then stopped as his gaze flicked over Baris and his expensive clothing.

"What are you doing here? You look like you should be over on High Street."

Baris had no idea what High Street was or what sort of clientele it catered to, but he didn't like the surly tone in the man's voice. The ale he had consumed had quickly gone to his head, making him dizzy. And the way the youth's eyes were darting about, as if unable to train on any one object, was not helping. Baris drew a deep breath.

"I will be where I choose to be."

The young man shrugged, then reached into his vest pocket. He took out a leather pouch and shook it in Baris' face.

"You have money, I have hack."

"What is hack?"

"Just the best thing since sex," the young man answered with a sly grin. "Just a pinch and you'll see the world in a whole different way. And my stuff's pure. It's not softened with some useless herb. You'll see the quality, taste the quality, feel the quality."

"A drug?" Baris shook his head. "I have no need for such."

"Suit yourself." The young man made to return the pouch to his vest but dropped it instead. With an oath he bent to retrieve it and stumbled, falling to his hands and knees. Broken glass sliced into his hand and he yelped, falling back to lean against the wall.

"Damn! Now look what you made me do."

Baris barely heard the words. His gaze was on the blood running freely down the man's hand and dripping into the dirt. His body began to respond with alarming intensity. There was something different about the scent of this blood, something alluring and powerful. Almost without thinking, Baris hunkered down before the youth. Without a word, he reached out, caught a drop of blood and placed it on his tongue.

The young man looked at him, his face screwed up in disgust. "What the hell are you doing?" he snarled.

Baris forced his gaze to the man's face, still reeling from the taste of the blood. He had never experienced anything like it. It rushed through his body, set his nerves to tingling, brought a giddy sense of well-being. He had to have more. He straightened and reached for the young man, who shrank back, confused and suddenly very afraid.

Baris smiled and let his Illusion fade away. The youth gasped, cloudy eyes going wide. Even in his drugged state, he knew what he viewed. He pressed back against the wall.

"No," he whispered.

"Oh, yes," Baris whispered back and clamped one hand at the youth's nape. His gaze locked on the man's and slowly, tauntingly, he bared his incisors.

"Please," the youth begged, though his voice was barely audible.

"Yes, you will please me," Baris returned and sank his teeth into the man's neck.

Chapter Thirteen

Baris looked up at the windows of the inn, then slowly climbed the steps. It was late afternoon, but what he had done with all of the time since leaving the inn that morning, he couldn't say. He couldn't remember. Now, his stomach rumbled with hunger and his muscles complained of fatigue. It was agony to drag his body up the long staircase to his room. He hesitated before rapping on the door. He had not thought to take his room key with him and wondered what he would do if Deirdre were out. Fortunately, she was there, dressed in her bedclothes, her hair rumpled, her eyes swollen and red.

Baris caught his breath. "What's wrong?"

"I...I thought you might not return," she managed, before once again breaking into soft sobs. She turned away from him.

He caught her and pulled her into his arms. "I'm sorry, Deirdre. I'm so sorry. I didn't mean to worry you. I didn't mean to hurt you." He lay his chin atop her head. "I'm sorry."

She said nothing for a few moments, just held onto him as if reassuring herself that he was indeed there. Finally, she spoke. "Where did you go? And why? Were you that angry with me?"

"Oh, Deirdre, I wasn't angry with you at all. I was angry with myself. Angry and disappointed. Anika was right. I needed to leave. I am not fit to be called her husband." He released her and sank into a chair by the fire.

After a moment, she came toward him and held out her hand. "Let me take your cloak. You look exhausted. I can make you some tea if you'd like."

He looked up at her, then took off his cloak. "Tea," he murmured. He remembered Quentin's words again. But it couldn't be. He had taken none of her tea for the past day or so. Still, he had been drawn to her, made love with her. Quentin had been wrong. It wasn't her magic that was controlling his actions. It was his lust. He nodded.

"Tea would be wonderful. After I rest a bit, we can go out for dinner. You must be starved."

"We don't have to go out, Baris. We can just eat here if you would rather."

"No, that's all right. There's a lot of city to explore out there." He drew a sudden, deep breath. Iron. "Have you been using magic?"

She flushed but nodded. "I was trying to find you. I was scared, Baris. I don't want to lose you. I...I love you."

He was somehow not surprised by her words. They only seemed to add weight to his already-burdened conscience. "Why don't you freshen up? I may not be good for much else but I can certainly heat water for tea."

Deirdre dropped down on the floor before him and caught his hands. "Baris, you are good for everything. You are kind, sensitive, sweet and so very much fun to be around. I couldn't help falling in love with you. Any woman would."

He chuckled harshly. "You make me sound like quite a catch."

She smiled and leaned forward to kiss him lightly on the cheek. "You are."

He looked into the dark depths of her eyes, then tenderly smoothed her hair. "Thank you, Deirdre. Your words mean more than you know. Now, go on, get ready for the evening. During my walks today, I saw that a play is being performed a few blocks from here. I'm going to take you."

She let out a soft gasp of delight, kissed him again and dashed toward the bathroom. "I'll be ready whenever you wish. And I'll make you proud, Baris. You'll see." She smiled at him, slipped into the bathroom and closed the door.

He sat staring at the door for a long time before rising to heat the water. His thoughts returned to the youth in the alley. He had left the boy weak and trembling but with a command to meet him near the inn later that evening. Baris knew the boy would honor that command. He had no choice. And Baris would be there as well. He wanted more of what this young man had to offer.

He went to the washbasin and splashed his face with cold water, then dried it vigorously. Deirdre's brush tamed his black locks. He wished he could see his own reflection, see what he looked like. All he had to go on was what other Vectors looked like. To him, they weren't all that imposing. But he knew to mere mortals they were.

On sudden impulse, he stripped, tossing his soiled garments into a corner of the room. He moved toward the wardrobe, intent on taking advantage of the inn's hospitality in providing new clothing. Deirdre's quiet, happy singing stopped him. He turned toward the bathroom. For a moment, he stood outside listening to her, then he turned the handle and stepped into the warm, scented room.

Deirdre looked up at him. "Baris?"

He approached the large tub, scooped up a handful of bubbles, then looked at her.

"Did you not invite me to join you the other night?"

She flushed and nodded. He blew the bubbles toward her gently. They floated through the air, landing on her head like a white, sparkly crown.

"Does that offer still stand?" he asked softly. Then, without waiting for an answer, he slid into the hot water behind her.

His hands found her breasts and he ran his fingers over their softness, even as she tilted her head back and his lips claimed hers. Gone was his indecision, his guilt, his conscience. He wanted her and he would have her. He nuzzled against her neck, his tongue drawing small circles in her warm flesh. He didn't need to feed, not yet, but he knew that she had used her magic. Still, he timed his penetration of her neck to coincide with the moment she turned to face him and he penetrated her body. Her gasp was intense, shrill; and she grabbed at him in desperation. He felt elated, intoxicated. Never had he experienced such an orgasmic rush. It claimed his entire body, left him gasping and dizzy. Finally, he lay, panting, his cheek resting on the edge of the cold metal tub. Deirdre's soft breaths brushed against his ear, sending chills dancing over him. He seemed unable to move, as if his limbs were made of stone, instead of flesh and blood.

Slowly, she began to stroke his back, her fingernails barely touching his skin. It sent shivers of delight through him, brought him to arousal yet again. Still, he was too exhausted to act on it. Instead, he closed his eyes and let her gentle touch lull him into sleep.

His rest was brief, but packed with nightmares. Faces swirled around him, jeering and taunting. Anika, Deirdre, Darius, Vail, Quentin, the young man in the alley. They all seemed to be laughing at him, as if they knew something he did not. Each time he reached out for one of them to demand to know what it was, they disappeared, fading away into nothingness, leaving him alone and frightened. In desperation, he turned toward Jaeger, silently begging the Vector to help him. But Jaeger only shook his head and turned away. Baris dropped his gaze and saw Thale. The little boy's eyes were full of tears, and anger reddened his small face. Baris held out his arms but Thale let out a wail and ran away from him. Baris tried to follow but could not. He could not move, rooted to the spot as if he were a tree standing alone in a meadow. And suddenly he became a tree, staring in despair at the forest beyond his reach, beyond his tearful pleas for acceptance. He was alone. He woke with a gasp and a cry.

Deirdre started, turning her head to look at him. "Are you all right?"

He nodded, though he was still shaken. "The water's getting cold. And if we're to get any dinner before the play, we need to get dressed." He climbed from the tub, picked up a towel and dried himself quickly.

Deirdre watched, her gaze sultry and provocative. "I like what I see," she murmured.

He glanced at her, some of his uneasiness fading. "Do you? Why don't you get out so we can compare notes?"

She laughed and did so. Bubbles slid slowly down her nude body, following each sensuous curve. She made no move toward a towel but gave Baris a small smile. "Why don't you dry me?" she purred.

Baris' body answered for him. He wrapped his towel around her and pulled her to him. Her skin was warm and moist, scented with the perfumed bubbles. It suddenly occurred to him that he smelled the same and he chuckled.

"What?"

"Nothing. It's just that people are going to be hard-pressed to tell which of us smells better tonight." He shook himself and backed away from her.

"We'd better get dressed or we may never leave the inn at all."

"And there's something wrong with that?" she called, as he left the bathroom.

Baris made no response but quickly dressed. He checked the water over the fire, then grimaced. It had almost completely boiled out. Carefully, he swung the hot pot away from the flames, then sighed. No tea. No magic. Just him and his amoral actions. He couldn't blame this on anyone, certainly not Deirdre.

"Deirdre," he called. "I'm going out for a moment. Just for some air. Be ready when I get back."

She appeared at the bathroom door, toweling her hair. She gave him a quizzical look but didn't protest. "I'll be waiting."

He smiled, his gaze once again absorbing her nude form, then he snatched up his cloak and left the room. He found the youth at the precise location he had ordered. The young man rose from where he had been sitting in the dark alley. Even in the absence of light Baris could see him quite clearly. He was still pale, still trembling, but he remained quiet as Baris approached.

A small voice screamed inside his head that it was too soon, that the youth needed time to recover that blood which he had already lost. But the voice was drowned out by this new need that surged through Baris' body. He wanted this youth, wanted his blood. But he didn't want to risk killing him.

"I never asked you your name," he said softly.

"Antyn," the young man answered obediently.

"Well, Antyn, I must repay you for your--gift. Please, follow me." He turned, knowing the youth would do as ordered.

They returned to the inn, where Baris purchased another room under his name, again using his Vector magic to preclude the need to dip into his nearly-vanished purse. He escorted the young man up the stairs and showed him inside the large, well-furnished room. Antyn took in the surroundings with one glance, then turned back to Baris.

"You will rest here," Baris said. "I will have dinner sent up for you. You will not leave this room unless I say you will. Is that clear?"

Antyn nodded. Baris licked his lips and approached the youth. His mouth watered at the thought of the man's blood and without further hesitation, he took what he wanted.

Chapter Fourteen

The next few days swept past in a blur. Baris was exquisitely happy but also agitated. He found it almost impossible to relax enough to sleep and spent a good portion of the nights either walking the city or taking blood from Antyn. He made love to Deirdre whenever he desired, no longer feeling any guilt for his actions. Thoughts of Anika were few and far between, thoughts of Thale even less. There were times when he wondered if they truly existed or if they had been merely part of his imagination.

He kept Antyn well-fed and well-rested, allowing him to go into the city during the day. What the youth did, Baris didn't care, as long as he was there at night so Baris could feed. As for Antyn, he seemed to be enjoying his newfound status. Baris doubted that he had ever lived in such splendor or eaten such exquisite foods. Baris even kept him well-supplied with hack, using his Vector magic to "buy" it from dealers. Antyn's addiction was pathetic to Baris' way of thinking, yet it was just one more hold that Baris had over the youth.

The only thing putting a damper on the situation was that Baris had long ago run out of money. True, he could still get what he wanted by using his Vector magic. There were very few humans who could withstand the power of his hypnotic suggestions. They willingly parted with food, clothing and goods with no mention of compensation. If Deirdre noticed, she said nothing. After all, most of what he procured was for her.

She now dressed in fine silks, wore expensive shoes, displayed jeweled hair clips and necklaces. No matter where Baris took her, what function they attended, she was the center of attention. Men flocked to her like bees toward honey, which both pleased and irritated Baris. She was his and he kept all others at arm's distance. They could certainly look but they couldn't touch. This seemed to be just fine with Deirdre. She made no pretense that Baris was anything other than her partner.

Still, there were times such as this, when he sat in the dark of night, that the nagging voice of doubt crept into Baris' thoughts. It seemed he should be doing something, going somewhere, but he couldn't clearly remember where. His mind seemed to be in a continual state of muddy confusion, his body always shy of being completely rested. He attributed his condition to his expending a good amount of his energy in magic use to attain the things he wanted. He had long ago forgotten Quentin's warning regarding Deirdre and her magic. He was settling into this city called Timmora and it seemed he would begin building a new life here.

He stood up, drained the last bit of wine from his glass and turned toward the door. Deirdre slept, exhausted from a day of shopping and an evening spent dancing. Baris studied her a moment, then leaned over and kissed her gently before leaving the room. He went straight to Antyn's room and entered without knocking. He was surprised to find the young man gone.

Until this moment, Antyn had done as ordered, keeping himself where his "master" could find him when the dark settled in. That he wasn't here sent irritation and worry through Baris and he turned his steps toward the streets. A cold wind blew through the city, picking up dirt and debris, sending little dust devils dancing through the night. Baris walked at a steady pace, pulled toward Antyn by his scent.

He found the youth in an alley, surrounded by four other men of varying size and age. One held Antyn by the hair while another pummeled his already-battered face. The other two laughed and encouraged the one beating their victim. Rage gripped Baris. He strode forward, his cloak billowing out behind him.

"Cease!" he bellowed, his voice ringing off the sides of the buildings.

The four men whirled as one. Antyn crumpled to the ground.

"Well," one of the men said, his voice thick and slurred. "What do we have here?"

"That's obvious," another man said. "It's Antyn's purse. And a fine-looking one, at that."

"Is the boy any good in bed?" another jeered.

Baris stopped before them, his fury barely controlled. "What is the meaning of this?"

The men laughed and one gestured at Antyn.

"His prices were a bit too high. We were negotiating."

"Prices for what?"

"Hack, what else? Think any of us wants to bed him?"

"Nah," another put in. "Antyn is yours, pretty boy."

The words snapped Baris into action. He gripped the speaker by the throat and lifted him completely off the ground. The man gagged, his eyes bulging and he clawed at Baris' hands in an attempt to free himself. The other three men backed away, their faces now shocked and frightened.

"Tell me," Baris growled, "why I should not kill you?"

There was a momentary pause, then one of the three men darted forward and buried his dagger in Baris' side.

"Because we're going to kill you first," he returned.

Baris' breath hissed out as pain flared through him. It took only a moment for his Vector magic to heal the wound, however, and then his tightly-held emotions exploded. He hurled the man in his grip against the side of the building with such force the wooden siding splintered. The man convulsed as he slid to the ground, dead.

"Who will kill whom?" Baris raged, fixing his gaze on the three men. They shuffled backward, their eyes wide with terror, as he shed his Illusion and let them see what they truly faced. He narrowed his eyes. "A pity that you will kill your friends, then yourself," he whispered to the one who had stabbed him.

The man went white. His hand lifted and he stared at it as if it no longer belonged to him. His two companions gaped at him and stumbled backward as he turned on them.

"No," one begged. "Come on, stop."

But he could not stop. He slashed with the dagger, opening the throat of the man nearest him. The other screamed in terror as blood spattered him. A moment later it was his own blood that stained his dirty clothes as he futilely tried to staunch its flow from his gaping neck wound. The man with the dagger managed to bring his gaze to meet Baris', but that was his last voluntary movement. He turned the dagger on himself, plunging it to the hilt in his chest. He fell with nary a gasp.

Baris drew a deep breath, almost overwhelmed by the scent of fresh blood. He bent and hauled Antyn to his feet. The youth was barely conscious. Blood covered his face and clothing. Several teeth were missing and blood and saliva oozed from his slack mouth.

"I told you to stay in your room after dark," Baris snapped, his anger overriding his compassion. "Now, look at you."

Only then did Antyn notice the four bodies. "You...you killed them!"

"They tried to kill me, too," Baris retorted. He dragged Antyn from the alley and back toward the inn.

The youth went with no arguing or struggling. The innkeeper looked up with a gasp as they came through the door.

"By the gods! What on earth happened to the boy?"

"He was waylaid and robbed by some of this city's more foul citizens," Baris replied.

"Shall I send for a healer?"

Baris shook his head. "No. My companion is a gifted healer. She will take care of his injuries. But, please, send up some soup and tea. That's about all he will be able to take."

The innkeeper nodded and hurried away. Baris helped Antyn up the stairs to his room. Once there, he locked the door.

"Get out of those filthy clothes," he instructed. "I will draw you a bath. Then you will rest and regain your strength."

"Why?" Antyn whined. "So you can keep taking my blood?"

Anger blazed up again and Baris stalked to where the boy stood. He stopped directly before him, forcing Antyn to tip his head back to look at him.

"Yes," he said quietly. "You belong to me now. Don't forget that. Get cleaned up."

The youth averted his gaze and stumbled into the adjoining bathroom. The soup and tea arrived while he was washing and Baris sat down to wait, then just as quickly got up again to pace. He stopped at the window and parted the curtains. All was quiet outside. He wondered what would happen once the bodies of the four men were discovered. He decided he didn't care. He would not be run out of a town again. Not for dispensing justice...even summary justice...to those who deserved it.

He turned and resumed his pacing. He realized he was trembling, his heart racing. His agitation was becoming uncomfortable. He needed to feed.

"Antyn!" he barked. "Be done." There was no answer. He rapped on the bathroom door. "Antyn!" Again, no answer. He turned the handle and opened the door.

Antyn sat on the floor, nude and still wet from his bath. His face was grotesquely swollen from the beating he had taken but his eyes were glazed and dreamy. He gave Baris a lopsided smile. Baris' gaze traveled to the pouch of hack lying on the floor beside him. It was evident that Antyn had used the drug to dull his pain. Baris grimaced, retrieved the pouch and placed it on the shelf outside the door. Then he pulled Antyn to his feet and near-dragged him to the bed. The youth toppled to the sheets with a little groan. He looked up at Baris through half-lidded eyes.

"Are you going to join me?" he slurred. "Am I your boy, Baris?"

Baris started. He sat down on the edge of the bed and with shaking hands pulled the boy to him.

"I want your blood, Antyn," he rasped. "Not your body."

"Are you so sure of that?" Antyn said and reached out to stroke Baris' crotch.

The touch ignited a strange fire within Baris, a fire he didn't know how to interpret. The scent of Antyn's blood was overwhelming him, calling to him. He needed it desperately. His body ached for it. He took a handful of Antyn's hair and pulled the youth's head to the side. The bite was quick and forceful and Baris drank deeply, totally consumed with his powerful, intoxicating response to Antyn's blood. It was a struggle to draw back, to stop the feed, but Baris forced himself away. He needed to save some for later. He needed to give the boy a chance to recover from his beating. He fell back onto the bed as Antyn's blood coursed through him, calming him, relieving his agitation, sweeping him once again to that place of well-being and peace.

Antyn smiled at him, kissed him gently on the lips, then slowly worked his mouth down Baris' throat and chest. Baris was too exhausted and euphoric to care. He merely closed his eyes and let Antyn do as he wished.

A persistent tapping on the door wakened him. It took him a moment to sort out his surroundings, but when he did, he groaned. Antyn lay curled up beside him.

"Baris!" Deirdre's voice came from the hallway. "Baris! Are you in there?"

Baris stumbled from the bed, noticing with a grimace that he was naked. He snatched up his pants and put them on before answering the door. Deirdre stared at him, her eyes widening as she took in the tousled hair, the bare chest and feet. She stepped into the room and swiftly closed the door. Her gaze went at once to the bed, where Antyn lay, unmoving.

"I'm sorry," Baris mumbled before she could say anything. "I must have fallen asleep. I'll get dressed."

"Have you been here all night?"

Her sharp tone made him defensive.

"Most of it. Why?" He picked up his tunic from where it had fallen onto the floor beside the chair.

"Because four bodies were found in an alleyway not far from here. I just wanted to make sure you weren't involved."

Baris grimaced, rubbing his throbbing temples. A little voice nagged in his mind, wondering how Deirdre had known where to find him, and why she so easily accepted the fact that he was in a room with a man. He forced himself to answer her.

"I'm afraid I was involved. I came on them as they were beating Antyn senseless. I stopped them but not before one of them tried to stab me." He touched his side where the wound should have been. All that remained was a faint red line.

Deirdre frowned and looked at Antyn. Her frown deepened and she crossed the room. A loud gasp escaped her and she whirled to face Baris. "Baris! He's dead!"

"What?" Baris joined her. He reached out and shook the youth. "Antyn?"

"He's dead, Baris," Deirdre repeated slowly, as though she wanted to be sure he heard.

"He can't be," Baris muttered. "He was fine last night. I mean, he was pretty well beaten but otherwise he seemed fine." He shook the young man again, his gut tightening in horror. His gaze shot to Deirdre. "I didn't kill him, Deirdre. I didn't!"

Her breath hissed out and she looked around the room. "But who's going to believe that, Baris. Look at his neck. You fed on him, more than once."

"But I didn't kill him," Baris insisted, though he could not clearly remember anything beyond the touch of Antyn's mouth on his lips, his chest, his-- He shuddered and turned away from the too-still body.

Deirdre stood quiet a moment, then reached down and pulled something from the blankets. It was Antyn's hack pouch. She opened it and sniffed the contents. "Is this his?"

"Yes. Why?"

"This is probably what killed him. He must have taken too much. He was probably trying to dull the pain from the beating but between that and your feeding he was too weak." She stared at the pouch thoughtfully for a long moment, then sighed. With a sidelong glance at Baris, she pulled the blankets over Antyn's head. "Come on. We have to get out of here."

"What? No! Deirdre, I can't just leave him here! I have to report this."

"And get hung for murder?" she snapped. She seized his hand and dragged him toward the door.

"But you said yourself that he probably died of an overdose. The hack in that pouch is proof."

"No," she snarled. "Those bite marks on his neck are proof. All of the proof a constable needs to condemn and execute you. Now come on."

Terror gripped Baris and he looked back at the bed. How could this have happened? How could things have gone so wrong? He returned his gaze to Deirdre, noticing that she still held the hack pouch.

"What are you going to do with that? You should leave it here so there's some sort of evidence."

"No. We're going to need this. You're going to need this."

"Why? I don't use that."

She regarded him as she might have done a child who had just said something incredibly stupid. "You're addicted, Baris."

He drew back, stunned at her accusation. "That's ridiculous. I've never even used that!"

"But you fed on Antyn and he did use it. It was in his blood and now it's in yours. We have to wean you from it slowly or you risk dying as well. Now stop arguing and follow me."

Her commanding tone irritated him but at the moment he could think of nothing to say or do in retaliation. He gave the dead youth one last glance, then followed Deirdre into the hallway and back to their room.

Chapter Fifteen

aris sat down on the log, shivering, then got up again. He wrapped his cloak tighter about his shoulders, only to loosen it again moments later. He couldn't decide if he was hot or cold, tired or full of energy, hungry or satiated. All he was sure of was that his head pounded unceasingly and that he craved the hack that Deirdre was safeguarding.

He let out a frustrated, angry sigh and glanced toward her. She ignored him, keeping her gaze on the meat roasting above the small campfire. He couldn't tell how she felt toward him right now, but he was plenty disgusted with himself.

They had left Timmora stealthily, creeping out like criminals. Deirdre had been forced to leave most of her finery behind so as to avoid suspicion at the amount of baggage she left the inn carrying. She was now dressed in the traveling leathers Baris had purchased for her, with her cloak thrown about her shoulders. Her hair was plaited, her glittering clips now relegated to the bottom of her pack. Baris' guilt was eating him alive.

"I'm sorry," he whispered. He closed his eyes and leaned his forehead against the nearest tree.

"I know," she responded, though he hadn't thought she would hear him. "You don't have to keep saying it."

He opened his eyes to look at her, stabbed by the hard undertone in her voice. "Do you think that..."

"No," she cut him off. "It's not time yet, Baris."

He grimaced and looked away. How could he want something so badly? How could his entire body demand a substance that before now had been foreign to it? He didn't understand. He supposed he could force her to give it to him, knew he could, in fact. But, as she had pointed out, it would not help him to do that. He had to be slowly weaned from the drug, given a set dose at set intervals of time. It was just that the wait seemed interminable. He pushed away from the tree and headed towards the woods surrounding them.

"Where are you going?" she demanded sharply.

"I don't know. Just for a walk."

She stood with a sigh.

"Baris, you need to rest," she said, her voice now free of the faint irritation he'd caught in it since they left Timmora. "You're exhausted. You're going to collapse. Come on. Back to the fire. I've made tea. That will take the edge off waiting." She took his hand and drew him after her.

He sat down beside her and accepted the tea mug. After a few sips, he looked into the amber liquid thoughtfully.

"Quentin told me that you spelled me," he stated bluntly. He brought his gaze to hers. "Did you?"

She let out a long, exasperated sigh. "We've been through this, Baris. I told you what I did. I made special teas to help you relax. I gave you extra tending for your depression and emotional upset. That's all."

He nodded. He did remember her saying that. More than once. He took another sip of tea.

"I've become a monster, Deirdre," he said softly. "You shouldn't be with me."

"A monster? Hardly. The men you killed were in the wrong. All of them. Antyn might be alive right now were it not for them."

Baris winced at hearing the name. He couldn't get the young man from his thoughts. "We shouldn't have just left him there. We should have notified someone. He deserved that much."

"You gave him more than he ever deserved." She was annoyed again. "He was a street thief. He dealt in illegal drugs. He was an addict himself. At least he's at peace now."

"I wish I was."

Deirdre gave him a wan smile then took the mug from his hands. She set it aside and straddled him, wrapping her arms about his neck. Her kiss was warm and gentle, stirring Baris' passion awake. He embraced her, burying his head against her shoulder.

"How can you still care for me after all that I have done?"

"What have you done, Baris? Protect me? Protect Antyn? You gave us both a chance to live a life we could only have dreamed about. I'm grateful and I'm sure Antyn was as well."

"I don't think so," Baris returned. "I made him a slave, Deirdre. He wasn't free to do as he pleased. He had to answer to me. I controlled his every move."

"If that were true, he wouldn't have been in that alley getting beaten up."

Baris had not thought of that. Still, it didn't negate any of the other facts. He had controlled Antyn. Had used his Vector magic to possess the youth. He hadn't known why at the time, though he did now. It was as Deirdre said. He was addicted to hack just as surely as if he had used it himself. Mere thoughts of the drug made his mouth water and he closed his eyes, trying to turn his mind to other things.

He was well aware of Deirdre's soft, warm breath upon his neck, of her curvaceous body pressed against his, of her slight movements meant to arouse him. But he simply couldn't respond. His heart was too bogged down with grief, disgust and self-recrimination.

Anika. The name popped into his muddled mind at the same moment it escaped his lips. Deirdre jerked back as if she had been stung.

"Anika!" she snapped. "Anika!" She got to her feet, her face dark with anger. "After all that I have done for you, all that I have helped you with, you still think of Anika?"

He frowned, puzzled by her outburst. "She is my wife, Deirdre." As the words left his lips, they seemed to settle into his heart. His wife. It seemed he finally understood what that meant to him. "She is my wife," he repeated.

"Wife? She kicked you out, Baris! Remember? She told you to leave. She doesn't want you anymore. Can't you understand that?"

The words hurt and Baris averted his gaze. "I still love her," he whispered. "I still want to find her, to help her. I--still want to be with her."

An awkward silence fell over the two. Deirdre whirled and began shoving supplies back into the pack.

"Fine!" she seethed. "If you are still so devoted to Anika then I won't stand in the way. I hope you find her and get your cozy little love nest back together!" She threw the pack over her shoulder and stomped away.

Baris leapt to his feet. "Deirdre! Stop! Where are you going? You can't leave. I need you!"

She spun on him, dug something from the pack and hurled it his way. The pouch of hack fell at his feet. "All you need is that. It's the only friend you have now," she said and stormed away.

He stared after her in shock, expecting her to turn around at any moment. But she didn't and soon disappeared into the woods. He started after her then stopped. What did it matter? He could do nothing but hurt her further. He could never love her as she wanted, never become her mate. His heart was pledged to Anika for eternity. He glanced at the hack pouch, then bent and picked it up. His thoughts went again to Antyn. Was it possible his death wasn't an accident, that the young man had taken his own life with the hack? Had his despair been so deep that death was preferable to serving Baris? Was it just one more death to add to his conscience?

He sagged to the ground before the small fire, staring at the pouch. Slowly, he opened it and took out a small pinch of the ground leaves. Deirdre had said it was too soon but he didn't care. He placed the leaves on his tongue and let them dissolve. The response was almost immediate. His trembling stopped and he drew a deep steady breath. Now, he could think more clearly, could make some decisions on what he would do. He closed his eyes, delighting in the peaceful tranquility that flowed through him. If only he could stay like this forever.

He was wakened by Anika's soft voice. Confused, he sat up, blinking into the darkness surrounding him. The fire had long ago burned out but the effects of the hack were still warming him.

"Anika?"

"Baris." The voice seemed to carry on the breeze that rustled the treetops.

"Anika? Where are you? I can't see you."

"Baris." The voice wrapped around him, caressed him, stroked his face and neck. He shivered, reaching out as if he could grasp it.

"Ani," he whispered. "I'm sorry. I'm so sorry I hurt you. Please, Ani, please forgive me." He shook with his sobs as tears trickled down his pale cheeks.

There was no answer and Baris felt the presence leave him. He sighed, lay back down and stared into the cold ashes, the pouch of hack clutched to his chest.

When he next woke it was to the light of mid-morning. A misty rain fell, bringing a chill that seeped into his very bones. He shuddered and drew his wet cloak tighter. There would be no chance of restarting the fire and he rose, grimacing at the stiffness of his joints. He was hungry and thirsty, but saw no source of water other than the rain. He cast his gaze about, looking for a plant where the precious liquid might have gathered. He found it in a broad-leafed flowering shrub. He hunkered down and carefully tipped the leaf, letting the small stream of fresh, cold water flow into his parched mouth. It took several more leaves to quench his thirst but at last he straightened.

He had no clear idea where he was. When he and Deirdre had fled Timmora, he had not paid attention to their direction. He had been too upset over Antyn's death to notice much of anything. That, and the effects of the drug, had left him hopelessly confused. Now, he regretted not being more alert. He glanced up at the gray skies with a frown. He had never been good at reading the skies, not even at night. And here in the thick forest, with no hill to afford a territorial view, he had no idea which way to walk, which way was north and Nowles.

He needed to clear his muddled thoughts, to focus. He knew what would allow that. He opened the pouch and placed a pinch of the leaves on his tongue, then stood still waiting for the euphoria to claim him. He frowned when it didn't. Maybe the leaves had gotten wet. He examined the pouch carefully, but found no tears or holes in the leather. He shook out a small amount of the leaves...they were dry. Frowning, he placed another pinch onto his tongue and waited.

Finally, the euphoria washed over him, soothing him, easing his anxiety, calming his muddled mind. He sighed with contentment and replaced the pouch inside his tunic, where it would stay dry and safe. All right, so he didn't know which way was north. And he risked stumbling back into Timmora. He couldn't stay here, in the middle of the forest, with no food or drink. He had to find a town. If Timmora were the only one nearby then it would have to do. Without Deirdre along to identify him to others, he could enter the city in any number of Illusions. The thought actually pleased him. Timmora was a huge city. A man could stay lost there for a good long time. There were plenty of places he could satisfy his need for blood as well. And, he thought with a small smile, he could get more hack there. He began walking with an urgency of step, his mind focused on returning to the very city he had just run from.

As he walked, his thoughts returned to the events of the previous night. Had it really been Anika's voice calling to him? Or had he only imagined it? Was it merely the dream of a grieving man? He reached up to touch his cheek where the wind had brushed against it the night before. Had that been Anika's gentle touch? If so, that meant she was looking for him. But why? To find out where Thale was? To force him to take her to the Lair? To beg him to return?

He snorted at the last thought. Why would she take him back? After all he had done? Memories flashed through his mind like sunbeams through swaying tree branches. They brought him nothing but more grief. The man in the alley who had attacked Deirdre, the four men who had beaten Antyn, the youth's resigned face, the man at Quentin's party as he had fallen to the floor. And then there was Deirdre. Beautiful Deirdre. She had helped him, encouraged him, loved him. And his actions had forced her away, too.

He stopped walking, suddenly too fatigued to continue. He lowered himself slowly to the dry ground beneath a heavy-branched fir, then rubbed the water from his face. Another small pinch of hack took the gnawing hunger pains away. He shook the pouch, analyzing how much of the drug was left. Not much. Antyn must have used a great deal in his attempt at dulling his own pain. Or committing suicide, whichever had been the case. Baris knew he needed to get to Timmora, find another source of the drug. He decided that he preferred to get it through a user's blood rather than ingesting the leaves themselves. Taking it through a feed seemed to intensify the effects and he could accomplish two things at one time. He leaned his head back against the tree trunk and closed his eyes.

Yes, that was what he would do. Return to Timmora and disappear into the darkness of the city. The thought pleased him and he slept for a time.

Baris walked the cold woods for two more days. He picked berries or munched on fern leaves to stave off the intense hunger pains that eventually even hack could not thwart. He saw no signs of Deirdre. What surprised him was that he also harbored no concern about her condition or whereabouts. He simply accepted the fact that she, too, had left him.

His supply of hack was dangerously low and he had been attempting to slow his intake of it but it seemed the less he took, the more he craved it. It was the only thing that got him moving in the morning, gave him the energy to keep going in the hopes of finding Timmora. It was the only thing that kept him warm at night and consoled him in his nightmares and loneliness. It was as Deirdre had said. It was his only friend now.

He had not even tried to access his Vector magic. He hadn't fed for days and was too exhausted and weak to even think about pulling the magic. He had not heard Anika's voice again, nor felt her presence, which only added to his despair. His mood had deteriorated into one of anger, disgust and grief, and he stomped through the woods daring anything and anyone to get in his way. Nothing did.

Finally, at mid-morning of the third day, he found a river. Relief coursed through him and he hurried to the bank to drink. The water was cold and fresh and he gulped great mouthfuls of it. His empty stomach churned at the onslaught of sudden substance and returned the offending liquid. Baris retched again and again, then fell to the ground in a cold sweat. He lay still, shivering, for a few minutes, then sought out the hack pouch. He opened it with trembling fingers and reached in. His fingers brushed against the bottom of the pouch, finding no leaves. Panicked, he sat up and tipped the bag. A solitary leaf, no bigger than an ant, fluttered out. It caught on the breeze and drifted out over the river and away. Baris watched it in disbelief. With a roar of anger, he hurled the pouch after it.

He didn't need it. He didn't need anything. He staggered to his feet and stumbled alongside the river, following it downhill. Twice he had to stop to heave and rest but he forced himself to continue. He was convinced that this river would lead to Timmora. It had to.

By late evening, he had given up. His trembling was so bad he could barely walk and the cold seemed to penetrate to his very soul. At the same time, hot flashes plagued him, leaving him wet with sweat, which then further chilled his body. He found a sheltered spot under a giant fir and lay down, pulling his dirty, wet cloak around him. There was no place else to go, nothing left to do. It was time for death and Baris wondered how long it would drag out because of his Vector blood. He had been told that there were few things that could kill a Vector. Poison, fire and drowning were the three he knew about. He had none of the first two, but there was always the river. In his weakened state, he was sure he would never last the rapids. But drowning? Just the idea made him shudder. He cast his gaze about for berries. He remembered from his youth someone telling him that red berries were often poisonous. Should he find some and ingest a handful? What if they did nothing more than make him sicker? Besides, he didn't have the strength to go looking.

He closed his eyes and let his thoughts drift to his wife and son. He brought up mental images of their faces, tried to remember how it felt to hold them, tried to hear again Thale's sweet little voice calling him Papa. All was lost to him forever and he could not stop the tears that spilled from his eyes and left streaks in the dirt beneath his cheek.

"Ani, Thale," he moaned aloud. "I failed you. I am so sorry. Know that I love you both with all my heart."

Toward morning, he heard movement on the other side of the brush. He sat up slowly, his head spinning, and peered through the tangled branches. In a few moments, a middle-aged man leading a donkey ambled down the path almost directly toward him. The traveler sang quietly and carried an axe, though it dangled loosely from a leather loop at his waist. His hat was tipped back on his head, shadowing a tanned and well-wrinkled face.

Baris had not fed for days and the sight of the bulging veins on the man's neck called to him. He took a deep, slow breath, struggled to his feet and stepped into the man's path, blocking him. The man stumbled back a step then tipped his head in greeting.

"Mornin'," he said, grimacing.

"Good morning," Baris returned. He could only guess at what the man saw. Baris had been days in the woods, with no bath, no clean clothing, no food. He was filthy, gaunt, and weak. But even in his emaciated state, it took Baris only moments to hypnotize the man. He approached slowly, his breathing rapid. The man remained rooted to the spot, his gaze fixed on Baris'. A second later, Baris had him. He drank deeply and drew back satisfied, though not satiated. Thoughts of hack raced through his mind. If this man was out here, looking so fresh and well-tended, he must not have been traveling long. A village should be nearby. A village with a tavern district, and hack.

"Where are you from?" Baris asked.

"Er...Erster," the man managed, though he swayed dizzily.

"Erster?" Baris looked past him as if the village would materialize in the forest itself. "How far is it?"

"A league or so. Not far."

Baris looked back at him. "Can I get hack there?" He felt shame at the terrible hunger in his voice when he asked the question, but he pushed it away.

The man averted his gaze. "Why? I...I don't know nothing about that stuff. I done nothing to break any laws."

Irritated, Baris shook him. "I am not the law. I simply want to know. Can I get hack in Erster?" When the man failed to answer, Baris' irritation blossomed into anger. Without another word, he pulled the man to him once again and took all the blood he needed and craved. He left his victim lying in a pitiful heap alongside the trail. He didn't even check to see if the man was dead or alive.

Baris entered Erster not more than an hour later. It wasn't as large as Timmora but he guessed it would serve his purposes. He could get lost in the teeming populace and he was certain that he could find hack in the dark alleys. He studied the men he could see from his place of hiding, then

Illusioned as a contemporary and headed directly to the tavern districts. It didn't take him long to find a person selling hack, a young man not much older than Antyn had been. Four other, middle-aged men huddled around him in the dim light of a back alley. Bins of rotting garbage fouled the air and rats scurried back and forth, oblivious to the business going on about their furred heads. Several drunks were sprawled in the dirt and debris, eyes closed, bodies twitching in unknown dreams or delirium. Baris picked his way cautiously toward the young man and waited for the other buyers to disperse before he approached. The young man looked up at him, obviously startled by his sudden appearance.

"Can I do something for you?" he asked, his tone wary.

"You can sell me what you sold those others."

"Sold?" The youth glanced about, then shrugged. "I'm not sure what you mean, sir."

"No?" Baris tightened his jaw in anger, fixing his gaze on the youth's eyes. "Tell me, do you use the hack or just sell it?"

The youth drew back, his face going ashen. "I...I...no, I don't use it," he managed. "I...I don't sell it..." He broke off at Baris' guttural growl and backed away. "Please, sir, perhaps you are lost. Your clothing suggests that you should be..."

"Enough!" Baris roared. Understanding gripped him. He had mistakenly Illusioned as an upper-class citizen of this town. It was apparent that this youth sold only to those he knew. Baris decided to use his wealthy appearance to his advantage. "I am prepared to pay well. I need the drug to assist a friend of mine. He is in exquisite pain and cannot get relief from anything the healers have to offer. I was told that hack might afford him the peace he seeks. I was also told that you had a pure form. Am I mistaken?"

The young man hesitated a moment, studying him.

"I have nothing on me," he said slowly. "But I can direct you to someone who might."

Baris swallowed his growing rage. "Then I take it that you have no desire to make money yourself?"

"Money is always welcome," the young man said. "But I do like to come by it honestly."

"And you were selling these four men what?"

"Tobacco, sir. Just tobacco."

Baris exploded. He gripped the young man by both wrists.

"I say different. You will give me what you have. Now." His gaze bored into the young man's. The youth's eyes grew wide, his mouth slackened and he nodded numbly. Baris released one of his wrists and the young man reached into his tunic to pull out a large, leather bag. Baris snatched it away from him, opened the tie with his teeth and sniffed the contents. Satisfied that it was indeed hack, he released his grip on the young man.

"Thank you," he said calmly. "Now wasn't that easier than the alternative?"

"The alternative?"

Baris ignored the frightened question. "Don't you have someplace else you need to be?"

Without a word, the man stumbled away, his gait awkward at first, as if he were only just learning how to walk. By the time he reached the end of the alley, he had recovered from Baris' spell and broke into a full run, disappearing from sight. Baris waited only a moment before placing a pinch of the hack leaves on his tongue. They dissolved almost instantly. The euphoria rushed through him like an old friend and he leaned against the dirty stone wall with a sigh of relief. His knees buckled and he sank to the ground, closing his eyes in ecstasy. This was what he needed, this was his salvation.

He sat in the alley as the skies overhead grew darker, the air cooler. Finally, it was the rumbling of his stomach that forced him to his feet. He needed food and a place to stay. He forced himself to the end of the alley and peered into the crowded streets beyond.

The wide lane was littered with all sorts of degenerates, as well as some fairly decent-looking folk. He centered on them and watched where they went. Most seemed to be heading toward an establishment on the fringe of the tavern district and that was where he went.

It was an alehouse, at least three stories tall. Most likely it offered rooms as well as refreshments. Perfect. He climbed the three narrow wooden steps, crossed the porch and entered. Smells assailed him, setting his stomach rumbling once again. Plates on wooden tables were piled high with some sort of meat-and-potato mixture. Hot bread rested on long platters, and tankards filled to overflowing were stacked almost end-to-end along the bar. Baris drew a deep breath and approached the barkeep. The big-bellied man eyed him with distaste.

"What kin I get you?"

"I would like to inquire about a room," Baris said, raising his voice over the din of rowdy customers. "Do you let rooms here?"

The barkeep studied him a moment, then jerked his head toward an inside door. "Through there. Payne'll help you."

Baris tipped his head and went in the direction the barkeep had indicated. It was a smaller room, more like an entry. A narrow, tall counter claimed one wall. Behind it stood a small man with thinning hair and a long, pointed nose, and a look of perpetual distaste on his thin face. Baris stepped up to the counter.

"I would like a room, preferably one with a bath."

"We're full," the man said, without bothering to look at his roster.

"Check again," Baris said tightly.

The man stiffened. "I said we're..." He broke off with a gasp as his gaze met Baris'. Sweat beaded on his forehead. "I ...that is..." He reached beneath the desk and practically threw a key at Baris. "Room 300."

"Thank you." Baris spun and took the rickety stairs at a slow, calculated pace. It was only when he was well away from the innkeeper's panicked stare that he relaxed.

He clutched at his temples as his head reeled. He was in no shape to keep expending magic the way he was. He found his room, unlocked it and stumbled inside. It was large and as well-appointed as this section of town likely offered. Thick chunks of blackened wood lay in the hearth but Baris was too fatigued to light them. Instead, he looked toward the large, iron bathtub that stood discretely behind a partition.

The tub was empty, no coals lingering beneath it. The whole room smelled musty, as if it had been closed up for some time. Baris wrinkled his nose, threw off his cloak and slouched onto the wide bed. He brought out the pouch of hack and opened it. There was a goodly amount of the drug in the pouch but Baris didn't take any. Instead, he stared at the gray-green leaves wistfully.

Ingesting the leaves produced the peaceful tranquility he sought, but he could not forget the intensity of the feeling when the drug was mixed with human blood. That was what he wanted, what he craved. But where would he find such? He rose and stepped to the window to peer into the dark streets below.

What he needed to do was find a user, someone he could befriend, feed on. He drew back from the window with a start of disgust. And kill. Another Antyn. He shook his head and rubbed his face. No! He wouldn't do it. Not again. He couldn't have another death on his conscience.

He turned toward the tub. He wanted a bath, then dinner, then a good night's sleep in a decent bed. He went to the tub and began to pump the water. It came out rusty and foul smelling, falling into a tub with at least an inch of dirt in it. Baris stared at the grimy water for a moment, then shook his head and once more sagged onto the bed.

How had he come to this? A filthy room in a rundown inn in a town where he knew no one? Tears pricked his eyes and he brushed them away with a shaky hand. Once again, he sought out the hack pouch. A large pinch of the leaves removed his despair and he fell backward on the bed to sleep.

He was wakened by a soft rapping on his door. Confused and groggy, he struggled to his feet and stumbled across the room to answer. A young woman stood in the hallway holding a stack of towels and a robe. She gasped when she saw him but held out the linens.

"For you, sir."

Baris realized that he had neglected to restore his Illusion. He took the articles from her with a tip of his head. "Thank you. What I would really like, however, is a decent place to bathe. The water runs foul."

A blush covered her cheeks. "I know, sir, and I am sorry for that. There are public bathing pools just a few blocks from here where the water is clear and clean. I could point you in that direction, but--"

"But?"

She fidgeted nervously. "I...there...well, there are better inns further into town, sir. Perhaps you would be more comfortable there."

He regarded her somberly. "And why would you suggest such a thing? Is your employer eager to be rid of me?"

Her blush deepened. "Oh, no, sir! That's not what I...oh, no, please don't think that! It's just that you...never mind. Forget I said anything. I'm sorry." She backed away, her eyes shining with tears.

Baris reached out and took her by the arm, stopping her.

"It's all right," he said softly. "I am new to Erster and I took the first inn I saw. Perhaps you are right. I would be more comfortable at another place." He hesitated. "My name is Baris. Yours is--?"

She paused, her gaze drifting to where he still held her wrist.

"Ella," she murmured, her voice suddenly soft and a little dreamy. Her tongue came out to caress her lips, though she kept her gaze averted. "I was told that you...well, Berg said that you might have--"

"Hack?" Baris interrupted, reading through her hesitation.

She brought her gaze up to his with a start. Only a slight nod of her head indicated her answer. Baris smiled and drew her into his room, closing the door quietly behind her.

It didn't take him long to settle into his new life in Erster. Ella was more than happy to exchange her blood for his hack. It seemed an equitable partnership. Yet, each time he fed, he was reminded of another partnership, which seemed to be buried deep within his mind. He simply could not bring it forward. Faces and names swirled through his thoughts on a continual basis but he could not put them together no matter how hard he tried. Not that he made it a priority.

No, his main goal was to keep Ella well supplied with hack, something that was proving to be increasingly difficult. The more he imbibed of her drug-laced blood, the weaker his magic became. It was becoming harder and harder to convince others to answer to his needs without money being involved. And money was something he had none of.

Ella kept him supplied with food, clothing and company, but he refused to allow her a place in his bed. He couldn't explain either to her or to himself why. All he knew was that there was a name attached to his reluctance...Anika. He could not clearly remember who she was but at the same time he knew she had meant a great deal to him at some point.

And there was another woman as well, a woman with dark hair and eyes, who figured prominently in most of his dreams, who seemed to continually overshadow Anika, to push her aside whenever his thoughts drifted there. The whole situation was uncomfortable enough that Baris attempted to sidestep it. Most of the time a larger share of Ella's blood would do that for him. On occasion, however, there was nothing that could stop the intense heartache that gripped him, the despair that threatened to overwhelm him. At those times, he walked the dark streets, alone and in pain. Though he had been attacked twice during such walks, his attackers had not lived to brag about it. Baris had quickly learned that death in the tavern district was forgotten even before the warmth had left the body.

It was during one of these nocturnal strolls that he spotted a familiar face. At least, he thought it was familiar. There was enough sense of recognition that he followed the young woman, keeping to the shadows for fear of being seen. She had left a teashop and was heading with purpose back toward the nicer district of town...a place Baris had learned to avoid. Now, however, his curiosity piqued, he followed her. His filthy clothing and disheveled appearance garnered him numerous looks of disgust, though no one tried to stop him. He watched as the young woman skipped lightly up the steps of a fine hotel and disappeared inside.

For long moments he stood in the dark of an alley and watched the building. He knew he should turn around and go back to his own world, to Ella and her tainted blood, but something stayed his movements. He knew this woman, and he was determined to find out how. He had only enough energy to Illusion his face, not create a pleasant appearance otherwise. Drawing a deep breath, he pushed away from the wooden wall and crossed the street to the inn. He was stopped as he stepped into the foyer. Two uniformed men approached him, hands touching dagger hilts.

"Please, sir," one said. "You must leave at once."

Baris narrowed his eyes, his anger surfacing easily. "And why is that?"

They refused an answer, closing in on him from each side.

"Come, sir, let us escort you back outside," one said in a quiet voice. He took hold of Baris' arm.

Baris jerked away. "Do not touch me!" he snapped. "I came here to visit an acquaintance."

The guards glanced toward the desk clerk. He raised one eyebrow.

"If you would tell me your acquaintance's name, I will send a boy up to fetch them."

Baris frowned. "I...I don't know her name. I was never properly introduced."

The desk clerk grimaced and flicked his hand at the guards. "Take him back to the gutters where he belongs."

The words sent anger boiling through Baris, but when the guards once again took hold of his arms, his rage exploded. He struck out at both men, flinging them across the large foyer as if they were mere toys. One landed hard on an ornately carved chair, reducing it to rubble. The other hit the desk and toppled over it, crashing into the desk clerk. Both sprawled to the ground.

The desk clerk snatched at a whistle that hung about his neck and began to blow. Piercing shrieks split the air, searing through Baris' tortured mind. He brought his hands up to cover his ears even as the two guards regained their feet. They approached from both sides, weapons drawn. Confused and disoriented, Baris backed through the open door and onto the wide porch.

More uniformed men were approaching, weapons flashing. They were all yelling, gesturing wildly, and Baris realized that they were coming for him, attempting to surround him. He leapt from the porch to the street, sending citizens scattering with shrieks of terror. His gaze darted about, seeking an avenue of escape. He found it in the alley at the side of the inn.

Without another thought, he spun and bolted into the darkness, the pounding feet of his pursuers thundering through his head. He would never escape, not in his condition. He was running blindly, this area completely unknown to him. He stumbled to a stop at the road's end, his breathing tight and painful. He had to shift, had to become something that could escape the men's wrath. He closed his eyes and pulled forth the magic that he had not used for so long.

It came grudgingly, but it came. In the space of a heartbeat, Baris the Vector became Baris the wolf and he tore away, seeking the safety and sanctuary of the forest beyond Erster. He ran until he could run no longer, then found a hollow tree and collapsed within, returning to his Vector form unbidden. His legs trembled, his body shook and his stomach upended numerous times before he lay still, beaded with sweat and shaking. His gaze swept past the forest canopy to the stars in the sky beyond. His situation was all too familiar. But this time, he vowed he would stay where he was and let death find him.

Chapter Seventeen

A gentle hand caressed his brow, brought a mug of hot liquid to his lips. He sipped at it tentatively, then gagged and coughed.

"Slowly," a soft voice said. "We want to keep it where it belongs."

Baris forced his eyes open, but his vision was so blurred he could not make out the face of the person hovering over him. Deciding it was only a dream, he closed his eyes again and relinquished himself to sleep.

He woke next in excruciating pain. His entire body seemed to be on fire. Every nerve sparked with agony, sending him into convulsions. Again, gentle hands held him, kept him from hurting himself as he thrashed blindly, trying to escape the searing pain. It seemed to be an eternity before the convulsions ceased, leaving him weak, dizzy and gasping for breath. And again he slept.

The cycle repeated itself several times, until Baris thought he could no longer bear it. He heard himself begging for first hack, and then death, anything to put an end to his torment. The soft voice reassured him, telling him that he would get through this, that he would survive. It would just take time, but the agony would end.

And, finally, it did. He opened his eyes to mid-afternoon light, able to focus for the first time in days. He stared up at the canopy of forest high overhead, at the blue sky beyond and thought he had never seen anything so beautiful. Birds chirped and called in the distance and he heard the skittering of squirrels as they raced along tree branches intent upon their own business. A soft breeze blew, bringing a fresh green scent and the pungent smoke of a campfire.

Baris took a deep breath, then turned his head. The action sent little waves of pain and dizziness through him but it was nothing compared to what he had been through. When his vision stabilized he let out a gasp of disbelief. Vail, Baul and the young woman he had followed to the inn at Erster sat near the campfire, talking softly and sipping tea. They glanced over at his gasp and smiled.

"Welcome back," Vail said quietly.

"How...?" Baris croaked. "Where...?"

"Don't try to talk too much yet," Vail instructed. "I'll explain." He poured another mug of tea and helped Baris take a small sip. "This should help a little."

It did, though it burned all of the way to his stomach. Vail sat back and gave him a wan smile.

"What happened? No, don't answer that. I just told you not to talk." He sighed and raked one hand through his mussed hair, then glanced at the young woman as if seeking her help.

But Baris managed to croak out, "Hack."

Vail and Baul both started. "Hack?" Baul echoed. "That's what you were mumbling about then? Hack? No wonder you were so sick. You almost killed yourself. Where did you get started on that?"

"Timmora. It was an accident."

"A bad accident," Vail murmured. "You could have died here in the forest. You're just lucky Baul and I were in Erster instead of Terska. We were waiting for you, as a matter of fact."

"Waiting?"

"Yes. Deirdre told us that you would meet us in Terksa. We waited for several days and when you didn't show up, we decided to try to find you ourselves. We thought maybe we had misunderstood her. I guess we had."

Baris stared at him in confusion. Terska? No. She said she had told Vail and Baul to meet them in Nowles, not Terska, not Erster. He frowned.

"Where is Deirdre anyway?" Vail asked, with a grimace. "I have a few questions I would like to ask her."

"Gone," Baris mumbled, his eyes fluttering closed. "Just like Anika. Gone."

"Anika?" Vail asked. "What does she have to do with anything? What are you talking about?"

But Baris was too tired to answer and once more he slept.

He woke feeling much better, though he was chagrined to see it was now early morning of the next day. It didn't seem that he had been sleeping that long. He looked over at Vail and Baul, who were just rousing themselves. The young woman slept on, wrapped against the cold.

"It's your turn to get more wood," Vail mumbled to Baul.

"Well, it's your turn to make breakfast," Baul grumbled back. "And this time, try not to burn it." He stumbled off in search of wood.

A small smile touched Baris' lips, surprising even himself. He had forgotten what it was like to be lighthearted. Vail caught the grin and smiled.

"Well, that's a welcome sight. Feel like sitting up today?"

Baris nodded and, with Vail's help, managed to get into a semblance of a sitting position, propped against a large rock. Vail folded up his blanket and placed it behind Baris' back.

"For extra padding," he explained, then busied himself with the morning tea.

Baris watched him for a moment. "I want to thank you, Vail. You and Baul. I have to admit that I'm very embarrassed over the state I was in."

"How did you happen to come by it anyway? You said it was an accident. How?"

Baris hesitated, his gaze again sliding to the woman. Vail looked over at her, then smiled.

"It's all right. Honey knows who and what we are."

"Honey?"

"Aye, that's her name." Vail leaned closer to him. "And well-deserved it is, too."

Honey chose that moment to wake, rolling onto her side and opening her gray eyes. Eyes that Baris had looked into before. He gasped at the same moment she did. She sat up, the blanket falling aside to reveal an ill-fitting blouse that had shifted seductively during the night. Vail blushed and reached out to cover her breasts but her gaze was locked on Baris.

"Ye?" she breathed.

Vail glanced at Baris in surprise. "You know each other?"

Baris frowned, trying desperately to place her. It was Honey who answered Vail.

"Not really, no. He came to me father's eatery in Terska. That's all."

"Then you *were* there?" Vail asked.

Baris nodded. "For a time, yes." He suddenly remembered Honey's words at the inn. How she had offered him honey with his bread. He wondered if she would have followed through with her offer. Somehow, he doubted it. The thought almost brought a smile. Almost.

Vail grimaced. "I don't suppose you know anything about a man..."

"Yes," Baris interrupted. "I killed him. He attacked Deirdre. I reacted without thinking."

Vail exchanged a quick glance with Honey, who shrugged and brushed long, golden strands of hair aside.

"He was a thief and a swindler. He didn't deserve ta live."

Baris did not miss the venom in the words and he looked to Vail. The young man gave a slight shake of his head, indicating he did not wish to discuss it further. Apparently Honey did. She drew herself up, a flush on her cheeks.

"Aye, he attacked me as well. More than once. I was neh so fortunate as to have a powerful man come to my rescue against the foul citizens of that town." Her gaze slid to Vail and the hard look vanished from her eyes. "Until Vail."

This time it was Vail who blushed. He cleared his throat self-consciously. "I...I didn't do anything spectacular, Honey."

"Yes, ye did, Vail," she gushed, then abruptly wrapped her arms about his neck and hugged him fiercely. "Ye rescued me from oblivion and I love ye for it." She planted a long, wet kiss on his mouth, only deepening his blush.

This time, Baris could not contain his smile at the genuine affection Honey held for Vail. At the same time it brought pain to his heart as his thoughts drifted to Anika.

"You never answered my question," Vail said softly. "How did you happen to get involved with hack?"

"I...fed on a person who had it in his blood. That's how it started. Then, when he died, I continued to use it in its leaf form."

Vail looked over at him. "He died? How?"

"I killed him."

Vail started, nearly dropping the teapot. "You bled him to death?"

"No. Deirdre said he took too much hack. He had been severely beaten and was using it to ease his pain."

"Then why do you say you killed him?"

"I think she was wrong. I think he took his own life rather than be enslaved to me, to my will, my command over him. I didn't understand it at the time. I do now. His blood addicted me and I couldn't let him go. I needed him."

Vail was quiet a moment as he prepared the tea. "Do you think it was possible that he simply died of his injuries?"

Baris shrugged. "I don't know. He seemed all right when I took him back to the inn. I fed on him but I was careful not to take too much." He shook his head. "No, I think he killed himself to escape bondage." He shuddered, thinking of Ella and the possibility that he had enslaved her as well.

Vail looked up as Baul returned, his arms laden with kindling. The young Vector dumped the entire load near Vail.

"There! That should be enough to last until tomorrow morning." He looked at Baris. "You look better. How are you feeling?"

"That's a powerful question," Baris told him. "How do I feel? Weak, hungry, thirsty and, above all, foolish. I cannot believe that I allowed myself to fall into such a trap."

"Well, you might have had some help," Vail said with a grimace.

"What do you mean?"

Vail looked over at him. "You reek of witch magic."

Baris started. "Quentin said the same thing."

"Quentin?"

"A Vector Elder I met in...well, I can't remember where now. But he said the same thing. Deirdre said she was using magic to help me relax."

Vail snorted. "Relax? More like 'respond'."

Baris shook his head, confusion raging through him. "I don't know what you're talking about."

"She was seducing you, Baris, using love spells on you."

The words stunned him. "No," he protested. "No, she wouldn't have done that. She knows I love Anika. Why would she...? No."

Vail shrugged. "What's going on with you and Anika? You said she was gone. Gone from where?"

"From me," Baris said. He drew himself up. "Anika asked me to leave."

Vail gasped. "Leave? Why? She's madly in love with you."

"I don't know. I was attempting to take her to Jaeger and Rhiannon. I thought perhaps one of them could find out what ailed her. Then Thale...by the Sovereign! Thale!" His thoughts flashed suddenly to his small son, and grief tore through him, as memories suddenly assaulted him. "Thale got bit by a snake. I...I took him to the Lair. Ani ran away. I couldn't find her."

Vail frowned, exchanging a confused glance with Baul. "You couldn't find her? Why would she run away? That doesn't sound like Anika."

Baris sighed, rubbing at his face "I don't know. Anika...well, she'd been sick. She wasn't herself. That was obvious when she left Thale after he'd been bit. I could never have thought she would ever abandon her own child."

"This makes no sense," Baul said quietly. "The whole village knew of Anika's love for you and your child."

"A spell!" Vail cried and his eyes widened. "A spell! Of course! I'll wager anything Deirdre was behind Anika's sudden change."

"Deirdre?" Baris huffed out an annoyed breath. "Why must you keep accusing Deirdre? She has been nothing but kind, sympathetic and caring. She tried to help Thale when he was bitten but Anika wouldn't let her. She scryed for Anika numerous times but could never find her. She scryed for you and..."

"Told us to go in the wrong direction," Baul interrupted.

Baris looked at him. "Perhaps I was mistaken. Maybe she did say Terska. I was not thinking clearly most of the time. She took care of me, helped me."

"And spelled you," Vail repeated. "And I wouldn't be at all surprised if she didn't start this plan of attack months ago by working on Anika."

Baris nearly threw his mug at the young man. "Will you stop! I cannot blame Deirdre for my failures. They were mine. I did something to drive Anika away. It was me, not Deirdre. She doesn't even have that kind of magic. She made herself sick on numerous occasions trying to do things that she didn't have the power to do."

"Deirdre?" Vail gasped in astonishment. "Baris, Deirdre has more power in her little finger than I do in my whole body. She's extremely gifted. She can manipulate people with just a thought, make them bend to her will. I've seen her do it a dozen times. Add to that, she's a great actress. She can turn on the tears and trembling at the drop of a hat."

Baris stared at him, stunned, speechless. His gaze shifted to Baul, who merely shrugged, not knowing Deirdre that well.

Vail sighed. "Maybe you'd better tell me everything that's happened to you since leaving the village."

Baris nodded numbly. He reached out to grip Baul's arm. "First, though, will you do me a favor? Will you return to the Lair and check on Thale? I may have forfeited my rights as a father, but I still need to know that he's all right, that he recovered from the bite."

Baul nodded. "Certainly. Would you also like me to have Darius find

Anika?"

Baris hesitated. "Yes, I would. But tell him nothing, please. And tell her nothing. I just want to know that she's all right. I pray that she is."

"I'll be back shortly then," Baul said.

"Baul," Baris interrupted him before he cast his spell. "Please, don't tell her where I am. I need to sort all of this out before I speak to her again, if she will even speak to me at all."

"As you wish."

"And bring back breakfast," Vail put in.

Baul grinned and cast his spell, disappearing.

"Now then," Vail said, looking to Baris. "Start from the beginning and leave nothing out."

"Nothing?"

"Nothing."

Baris started with the attitude Anika had developed over the previous several months. "I don't know what it is, Vail. She refused to let me bleed her, even when she was ill. Yet, at the same time, she seemed to begging for my help."

"Explain that," Vail urged, his eyes narrowing.

Baris shrugged. "There were times when I saw the old Ani emerge. I could see desperation in her eyes, hear it in her voice. Then it would be gone as quickly as it appeared. She would turn away from me, discard me once again. That's why I left. I wanted to find you, perhaps get some answers."

"Why was Deirdre with you?"

"She simply wanted to get out of the village. That's all. She felt trapped. I can understand that, Vail. I have often felt the same way. I told her she could come along. And she was a great help with Anika and Thale."

Vail grimaced, but said only, "I see. Go on."

"Things are jumbled, Vail. I can't remember exactly how everything happened. I remember Anika running. I couldn't find her, no matter how hard I searched. Deirdre even helped me."

"How?"

"She scryed for Anika several times. It did no good."

Vail nodded, encouraging him to continue. "And the man Honey spoke of? What of him?"

"He attacked Deirdre," Baris said bluntly.

Vail grimaced. "Did he say anything in his defense?"

Baris thought a moment, then admitted the answer with difficulty. "Yes. He claimed she had paid him, that she had approached him, not the other way around. She denied it. And her dress was torn, her flesh abused. I had no reason not to believe her. I believe her still."

Vail sighed. "Go on."

Baris shifted uncomfortably. "We left the village soon after and found another. This one was quite a bit larger. I remember we brazenly walked into a party, became part of it. That's where I met Quentin. And where another man..." He looked up at Vail, his uneasiness increasing. "Another man wanted to take possession of Deirdre. I broke his arm when he tried to stab me. Quentin told us to leave. We did so the next day."

"This man who tried to stab you, did he say anything?"

Baris shook his head. "I don't remember. I just remember that he seemed entranced by Deirdre. He didn't want to relinquish her to me."

"Entranced? Or spelled?"

The question ate at Baris' gut. He continued. "I can't remember exactly where we went after that but we eventually ended up in Timmora. That's where I met Antyn. And where I became addicted to hack."

"Why did you leave there? Because of Antyn's death?"

"That and the other deaths I was responsible for." Baris rubbed his face, as if he could remove the horrible memories. "There were four men beating Antyn. I tried to stop them and one attacked me. I was so furious, I killed them all. But the hardest part is that I don't think I killed them for Antyn himself as much as for his blood."

Vail was quiet a moment. "Think back, Baris. What stopped you from using your Vector magic to return to the Lair and ask Darius for help?"

"I don't know if there was any one thing," Baris answered. "I just always seemed to have used up my magic and energy. I shapeshifted several times, once to save Deirdre from drowning in the river. She had fallen in and was washed downstream."

"Most likely she did it on purpose just so you would use your magic."

Baris shrugged, confused. "What are you saying? That she purposely found ways to keep me magically weak? So that I wouldn't return to the Lair?"

"Exactly. I'll bet she was plying you with her special herbal teas, too?"

Baris gasped and Vail grimaced.

"There you have it, Baris. You were spelled the entire time. Deirdre was using everything she had to make you hers. And she didn't care what it took to accomplish that."

"But why?" Baris breathed. "I'm nothing special. Why would she go to such extremes for me?"

Vail grinned. "Perhaps you're more of a catch than you think. It could be plain obsession, but knowing Deirdre, I think there was more to it." He paused, then went on. "I think it boils down to jealousy and retribution, Baris. And it goes a long way back. When we were younger, Deirdre fell in love with a boy named Ris. Unfortunately, Ris didn't share her feelings. He cared for Anika. They were quite a couple. They were always together, despite Deirdre's attempts to separate them. Ris had more than enough magic to thwart even the best of Deirdre's spells. Then one night, she asked him to meet her. He chose instead to be with Anika for a night of moonlight swimming. He dove in, hit his head on a hidden snag and drowned. Deirdre never forgave Anika for that. She claimed that if Ris had met her like she wanted, he would still be alive today."

"Anika never mentioned this Ris to me."

"I suspect she never will. It was too painful. She did blame herself for his death for many years. She may still. I don't know. The point is that when Deirdre saw how much Anika loved you, she was determined to hurt Anika as much as she felt she had been hurt by Ris. If Ris rejected Deirdre, then Deirdre was going to see to it that Anika lost you. If Deirdre could have you and flaunt it in front of Anika, so much the better."

Baris shook his head. "No. I cannot see how an incident that happened when they were children could make Deirdre do all of this. There has to be more."

Vail sighed and nodded. "Oh, there is. What did Deirdre tell you about her time away from the village?"

"That she was in school. Why?"

Vail snorted. "School? No. She was incarcerated, Baris. Not a jail like you're thinking. More like a--an asylum. She became so angry after Ris's death, so cruel and violent with her magic, that she was sent away, sequestered where she couldn't use her magic to hurt anyone. She only returned to the village when she had convinced the priests that she had reformed, that she had shed her anger. Just in case, the priests also ordered she be betrothed to Holt, because he was the only one deemed strong enough to handle her magic."

"Holt?" Baris stared at him, wide eyed. "But she said that her father had promised her to Holt. She detested the man. That was one of the reasons I allowed her to accompany me. I could not see her being forced into a marriage she did not want."

Vail shook his head. "Of course she didn't want it. Everyone thought that Holt had the ability to control her magic. Apparently he wasn't as strong as they hoped. He must not have sensed Deirdre's use of magic to spell Anika. Or you."

"But why Anika? Why me?"

"Because it was Anika's testimony, along with mine, that put Deirdre into the asylum. And you, you were an easy way out of the village. You had magic, strength, presence and the ability to keep Deirdre healthy. Not to mention that it was the perfect opportunity for Deirdre to get the revenge she so wanted on Anika."

Baris was silent as all of the information sunk in. Then, he shook his head. "But I killed for her," he whispered. "From what you're telling me, the man was innocent. I killed an innocent man and assaulted another."

"He was no innocent!" Honey put in vehemently, startling them both. "I can tell ye that."

Baris looked over at her. "But he was innocent of any crime against Deirdre."

"I'm sorry, Baris," Vail said. "Deirdre is ruthless when it comes to getting what she wants."

Baris covered his face with his hands. "And what of Anika? What would Deirdre have done to her?"

"I don't know. I don't think she would have killed her outright but I don't put it past her to allow it to happen. If she spelled Anika out into the forest--" His words drifted off.

Baris looked up at him but before he could say anything, Baul returned. The Vector wore a smile.

"You'll be relieved to know that Thale is fine. He's fully recovered and giving Darius a severe workout in trying to keep up with him."

"Thank the gods!" Baris breathed. "And Anika?"

Baul hesitated, glancing at Vail. "She's with another Vector, Baris. He's been caring for her for a few days now."

The words bit into Baris' heart and he dropped his head to keep the others from seeing his tears. "Then she's well?"

"I guess so. I don't really know her condition. Darius didn't say. I didn't press for answers."

"That doesn't mean anything, Baris," Vail tried to reassure him. "She's your wife. Isn't there some sort of Vector code that keeps one of you from intruding on another Vector's lifemate?"

"There is," Baul said.

"But there is no reason for her to honor that code," Baris pointed out. "It must be her choice. If she is happy, then I will not intrude. The only thing I will ask is that she allow me to see my son on occasion."

Vail and Baul were silent for a moment, then the latter spoke.

"Darius also found Deirdre."

Baris' head snapped up, his grief forgotten in a growing anger that he had been so thoroughly used by someone he had trusted. "Where?"

"In Timmora." He paused. "She was apparently trying to locate Anika."

Baris started. "Why?"

Vail grimaced. "Who knows? But with Deirdre it can't be good."

Baris struggled to stand. "I have to get to Timmora. I need to talk with Deirdre."

"I don't think you're in condition to go anywhere just yet," Vail said, rising. He reached out to grip Baris' arm.

Baris swayed, his head reeling. His stomach rumbled uneasily, threatening to disgorge what few sips of tea he had taken that morning. He knew Vail was right, yet the mere chance that Deirdre might do something to harm Anika drove despair through him.

"Listen," Vail said softly. "If you want me to, I can go after Deirdre."

Baris hesitated. He had heard all Vail had said regarding Deirdre's power but he was having a hard time believing it. And there was still an aching in his heart to hold her, to be with her, to make love to her again. He wondered how much of that was her spell and how much was simply his own treacherous desires. Yet, he also ached to be with Anika, to look again into her eyes, to hear again her soft words of love. He sagged to the ground, overcome with confusion.

"I don't know what to do," he whispered. "If Deirdre is as powerful as you claim, Vail, then I won't have you endangering yourself for me. At the same time, I don't want her to hurt Anika any more than she already has." He looked at Baul. "This Vector Anika is with, he should be able to protect her against Deirdre. She's probably safer with him than with me. Is there any way you can find out who he is? Where he is?"

"I suppose Darius would know," Baul said. "I could ask him. If you want, I could even pay the Vector a visit, check on Anika for you, let her know what has happened."

Again Baris hesitated. Finally, he let out a soft cry of despair. "But you don't know all that has happened. I've forsaken my marriage vows. I betrayed Anika. I was unfaithful. I can never expect her to take me back now."

Vail hunkered down before him. His words were gentle, completely non-judgmental. "Baris, listen. Whatever happened between you and Deirdre was of her doing. Anika knows her, what she is capable of. She will understand. I can promise you that."

Baris looked him in the eye. "But I can't convince myself that it was all due to Deirdre's spells, Vail. If you only knew the way I wanted Deirdre, the way I lusted over her, the..." He shuddered suddenly and pulled his blanket close, his gaze flying to Honey. "I'm tired. I need to rest."

Vail touched his arm. "I think what you need is to feed," he said softly.

Baris shook his head. "Not yet. Not on you. I can wait."

"Wait for what? For who?"

Baris shrugged and lay back down, closing his eyes. "I don't know, Vail. I don't know."

Chapter Nineteen

It took two more days for Baris to be able to stand for any length of time without help. Even then, walking was still only a wish. He managed two or three steps at a time, only to become rubber-kneed and sag back to his blanket. Vail assured him that he would get better but he was beginning to doubt it. His mind had returned to thoughts of hack, of the tranquility it provided, the energy. It didn't seem to matter to him that using it had placed him in this condition in the first place. His mind refused to see the horror of the drug and instead focused on the relief it could provide. He began to think of ways to slip away from Vail and Baul, get to Timmora and find someone to sell him the drug. Getting the drug filled his every waking thought and often intruded into his sleep. He needed it as surely as he needed the air he breathed. He could actually picture the large leather pouch lying in his room in Erster. He supposed by now Ella had claimed it, along with the few possessions he had managed to acquire. He berated himself continually for leaving such a valuable item in plain sight. He should have kept it on his person at all times. Yet, that night he had not been planning to follow a beautiful young woman so far from the tavern district.

He regretted following Honey, he regretted entering that inn, attacking the guards, running. But most of all, he regretted getting Vail and Baul involved in his sordid life. He found himself wishing with increasing frequency that he had simply died there in the hollowed-out tree. He supposed it was Baul who had sensed another Vector in the area, one in serious need of help. Baris was both grateful and irritated at his intervention.

His thoughts of Deirdre were as confused and rampant as his emotions. He loved her and despised her at the same time. He wanted to hold her and yet he wanted to punish her for what she had done to him and to Anika. And Anika! By the Sovereign! Baris didn't know what to think of her anymore. He was both happy that she had found a caring man and furious that she had. Again, he was left in total confusion by his inability to fully understand human emotions. If Anika loved him as she had proclaimed over the last few years, then why was it so easy for her to fall into another man's arms? The thought sent shudders of self-recrimination through him. Had he not done the same thing? Could he really blame all of his lustful actions on Deirdre's spells? On her teas? He didn't think so.

He still had not fed, despite Vail's urging him to do so. As a result, his sexual emotions were bottled up inside and he was now terrified to let them loose. He was sure he would take more from Vail than merely blood if given the chance. Honey had even offered to let him take her blood but Baris just couldn't add that to his already overburdened guilt level. With her beauty and gentle ways, he was positive he would take her sexually. And again, the mere thought disgusted him. He began to think of himself as nothing more than a vile degenerate who belonged in the gutters, as the Erster innkeeper had proclaimed.

Baul had gone back to the Lair but had not returned with any useful information. Apparently the Vector holding Anika was not willing to have his identity discovered, even by the Sovereign himself. Baris wondered how Darius was taking such an insubordinate action. Probably not well. On the other hand, Darius's rule was one of self-monitoring. As long as a Vector did nothing to endanger the race, they were free to pursue their own lives as they saw fit. If that meant breaking a Vector "rule" by claiming another Vector's lifemate, then so be it. As long as the lifemate was agreeable, Darius was unlikely to interfere. Especially if that lifemate were a mere human.

Baris rubbed his face and glanced toward his companions. They were all asleep and he knew he should be as well. The problem was he had slept so much in the past few days that he couldn't do so now. He sat up, holding back a moan of pain as his stiff joints protested the movement. For long moments he stared into the darkness beyond the small campfire, then pushed himself to stand. The fire was burning low. At least he could fetch more wood for it. He started away, his steps slow and awkward.

It was then he saw the apparition.

"Deirdre?" he whispered, then shook his head and closed his eyes. But when he opened them again she was still there, her form floating above the ground, a soft specter in the night.

Baris glanced at Vail, Honey and Baul, but they slept on. He turned back to Deirdre to see her motioning to him. He staggered toward her. She floated closer, reaching out for him. He felt the heat of her body as she wrapped her arms about him. He tried to hold her, but both could and couldn't. He was aware of her substance, yet his hands passed through her.

She pressed her lips against his. She tasted of mint and spices, and Baris melted into her embrace, returning her kiss with a burning passion.

"Baris!"

Vail's voice invaded the dream. Baris whirled, then spun back toward Deirdre. She was gone. He sagged and Vail caught him, preventing him from falling.

"What are doing?" Vail asked. "You shouldn't be up."

"It was Deirdre," Baris whispered. "She was right there."

Vail glanced toward Baul, who sat up near the fire.

"She was! I swear it. She was right there."

Vail sighed and led Baris back to his blanket.

"I don't doubt you. It's possible it was her image," Vail said. "I told you she has fairly powerful magic. She could have been scrying for you and allowed you to see her. And Timmora is only about three leagues from here. Her magic could certainly extend that far."

"But why? Why would she come here? Like that?"

Vail shrugged. "I don't know but I'm not comfortable with her knowing that Baul and I are with you."

Baris looked over at him. "Why not? She wouldn't do anything to hurt you."

Vail shrugged again but said nothing. Baris frowned and drew his blanket tighter about his shoulders. His gaze wandered back to the spot where he'd seen the apparition. His fingers touched his lips. He could still taste her kiss, still feel the passion that coursed through him. What was happening to him? Was he that possessed by Deirdre? Or was it merely more of the effects of hack? And what had Vail meant by being uncomfortable that Deirdre knew they were together? Would Deirdre really do something to the two young men? To Honey?

He shifted his gaze back to Vail and Baul. They had both once more fallen asleep, Honey wrapped securely in Vail's arms. Baris waited for a few more minutes then rose quietly.

He couldn't take any chances. While he seriously doubted that Deirdre could, or would, do anything to harm either Vail or Baul, it was not something else that Baris needed to weigh down his conscience. Silently, he slipped into the woods and melted into the darkness. It struck him as a bit odd that neither Vail or Baul stirred, when previously his slightest movements had roused them but he pushed that concern to the back of his mind and crept on. He knew exactly where to go, where to find Deirdre. He never even stopped to examine why he wanted to.

He walked until the sky began to lighten with the coming of morning. It occurred to him that he seemed to have plenty of strength and stamina all of sudden, when just prior to Deirdre's apparitional visit he could barely walk. More than once his fingers brushed against his lips, remembering the strange minty flavor of her kiss. Was it possible that she helped him? That she had somehow transferred healing to him through her touch? Once again, doubts rose up to plague him. How could Deirdre be as coldhearted and cruel as Vail painted her? All she wanted to do was help him, help Anika. Vail had to be wrong about her. He had to be.

By late morning, Baris was again exhausted. He leaned against a tree, his breath coming fast and shallow. He had not thought to bring any supplies, not even a waterskin. His throat was parched and raw. He needed food, water...and blood. He pushed away from the tree, intent on finding something to ease his discomfort.

Instead, it found him.

A young man, whistling softly, rode through the wood, careless of both mind and step. His horse nearly collided with Baris, who drew back with a gasp. Baris didn't even waste time or energy to Illusion himself. Surprisingly, the young man wasn't the least nonplussed by the fact that he had nearly run over a Vector. He reined in his animal and smiled at Baris.

"Are you Baris, by any chance?" he asked, his voice soft and slurred.

Baris stared up at him in astonishment. "H...how do you know me?"

The stranger slid from the saddle and cocked his head, now looking up at Baris, who towered over him. "Deirdre sent me. To find you."

"Deirdre? She sent you to me? For what? Why?"

The man chuckled and tapped two fingers against his neck. "I would suppose for this."

Baris was speechless. The man shrugged.

"'Course if you don't want it, that suits me fine, too. But I'm not giving back the money. It was your choice. You tell her that, will you?" He made as if to remount.

Baris held him back, his heart hammering. Yes, he wanted what the man had to offer. His mouth already watered at the mere thought. And the rest of his body was equally ready, much to his annoyance. He noticed his hands were shaking and he released his grip on the young man, only to just as swiftly take hold of him again.

The young man gave him an annoyed look and attempted to pull away. "You made your choice. Let me go."

"No," Baris mumbled. "I...I..." He dispensed with further words, took a quick breath and pulled the young man against him.

His bite was quick and efficient and he drank deeply. It took only moments for the strength to flow back into his body, seconds for the familiar euphoria to wash over him. He drew back, startled, staring in disbelief, then tore open the man's jacket. A leather pouch tumbled out, falling onto the ground, spilling hack into the dirt and leaves. Baris' gaze followed it.

Sudden anger tore through him and he looked back at the man's pale face. "No!" he roared.

The young man looked down at the spilled hack, his face twisted with annoyance.

"Eh, now, look what you've gone and done. Wasted it, you did." He looked back up at Baris. "You owe me for that."

Baris glared at him. "I owe you nothing. I owe no one anything!" He released the man with a hard shove.

"I say you do!" the man growled and abruptly whipped a dagger from his belt sheath. He brandished it menacingly, though his eyes were glazed, his gait unsteady.

Baris, held between rage and the euphoria of the drug, merely regarded the other for a moment. Then, with one swift movement, he disarmed him with such force it sent the young man flying through the air like a rag doll. He slammed against a thick tree and slid to the ground. Baris regarded him distantly, then looked back at the spilled hack leaves. He bent, retrieved as much as he could find, replaced it in the pouch and tucked it into his tunic. Then he straightened, mounted the horse and turned it toward Timmora.

He reached Timmora late that afternoon. Exhausted, he paused at the edge of town, his gaze moving over the citizens as they went about their evening business. He glanced down at his filthy clothing. He needed to see Deirdre but first he needed to clean up. He entered the first inn he saw and approached the counter. The innkeeper looked up at him, startled, his face going white.

Baris caught the man's wrist in a tight grip and fixed his gaze on the man's eyes.

"A room," he commanded quietly. "With a bath. And send up fresh clothing in my size."

"Your size?" the man blubbered. "But I...I.."

"Take a guess, but be careful you're very close," Baris snarled, then tapped the counter with his other hand. "A key. And your silence."

The innkeeper nodded and fumbled beneath the counter. He procured a heavy iron key, which he slid toward Baris. Baris smiled, picked up the key, released his grip on the man and strode toward his room. Once there, he lit the fire under the tub, then sat down to wait for the water to heat. Without a conscious thought, he drew out the leather pouch. A pinch of hack cleared his thoughts. His plan seemed simple enough. Find Deirdre and verify all that Vail had told him. Now that he was no longer under her spell, he should be able to see things as they really were, not as she wished them to be.

His anger grew as his memories washed backward. All that Deirdre had put him through, all of the immoral and horrible things he had done, came back to haunt him. Yet, there was still a part of him that could not believe it all, could not believe that Deirdre was the manipulative woman that Vail painted her to be.

Well, in a few short hours he would know. He rose and stripped off his filthy clothes. The water was barely warm but he ignored that and scrubbed clean, wishing he could wash away his guilt as easily as the dirt. He found a new set of clothes hanging on the outside of his door and quickly brought them inside to dress. Once again looking presentable, he Illusioned himself as a middle-aged man and strode from his room.

His first stop was the city cemetery. It wasn't hard to find the fresh graves, and he stood over Antyn's for a long moment. A simple wooden marker bore only the young man's first name and date of death. Apparently not much else was known about him. Baris turned his steps toward the stonemason's shop on the edge of the cemetery. The aging mason looked up at him with a welcoming smile.

"That grave over there," Baris said quietly. "The one marked 'Antyn'. I would like a stone carved for it, please."

"Yes, sir." The mason took up a parchment and quill. "What would you like it to say?"

Baris paused, thinking. What could he say? What right did he even have to put last words on the youth's final resting place? He drew a deep breath.

"May God accept his tortured soul," he finally said. "May he rest in the peace he sought."

The mason jotted down the words then looked up at Baris as if to ask for payment. Baris grimaced and once again used his magic to coerce the man into doing the task for free. The mason nodded and Baris left the shop. He turned toward the finer section of town, vowing that he would return to this place and properly pay everyone he owed.

He allowed his Vector instincts to guide him toward the inn in which Deirdre had sought refuge. The innkeeper remembered her well. It took but a touch of Baris' magic to gain an extra key to her room. He hefted the iron key thoughtfully as he climbed the stairs. He wasn't sure what he would say to her, how he would approach her. He knew only that he had to verify her power, had to see for himself just what she was capable of. He paused outside her room, then fit the key in the lock and turned it.

Deirdre whirled to face him, her eyes wide. "Baris!"

He stood still in the doorway, his senses tingling. The room reeked of iron. The scent almost overwhelmed him. It filled his senses, brought hunger to his mouth. His gaze swept over her.

She was beautiful. She wore a pale yellow silk dressing gown, one Baris had never seen. It accentuated her curves perfectly, barely able to contain the creamy mounds of her breasts. Her dark hair was piled loosely atop her head and jeweled clips caught the firelight. His body once more responded to her closeness. He closed the door behind him.

"Hello, Deirdre."

A smile of relief crossed her face as she approached him. "I'm glad you came," she whispered. "I missed you."

"I...I missed you, as well." He looked down at her pale face, her heavy-lidded eyes. Her need to be bled was acutely apparent. He suddenly felt weak-kneed and sagged onto the large bed.

"Oh, Baris." She stood close in front of him and gently smoothed his tousled hair. Tears shone in her eyes. "I'm sorry I left you. I...I was just so hurt and angry. And then--I looked for you but I couldn't find you. Finally, I had to stop. I was just so tired, Baris. So very tired."

He drew a deep breath, savoring the scent of the iron, letting his arms wrap around her and pull her closer. His planned words fled him, thwarted by the softness of her voice, the gentleness of her touch.

"I'm sorry if I hurt you, Deirdre. I never meant to."

"I know that now. I was being foolish."

"You...you haven't been bled," he whispered, embarrassed and yet thrilled by the hunger.

"No. I couldn't. Every time I tried, my thoughts went to you. I wanted only you to touch me." Tears trickled down her pale cheeks. "I need you, Baris. I need your help now." She pulled away and looked into his eyes. "I thought you might need mine but I can see you have been taken care of, just as I'd hoped."

"Oh?"

"I was worried about you, Baris. I sent several men into the woods to find you. I didn't know if you had been able to feed. I didn't know if you even could get to a place where you could find what you needed."

"You sent that man?"

"Yes." Her face brightened. "I take it one of them found you."

"Yes, one found me, but I wish I had known he had hack in his blood before I fed on him."

Deirdre frowned and bit her lip, her face the very picture of annoyance and frustration. "I should have known better. He vowed he wouldn't use it himself. He said he never touched it."

"Why did you send him with hack, Deirdre?"

Her frown deepened. "I...I thought you might need it, Baris. I wasn't sure how much you had. I...I didn't want you to suffer."

Baris studied her for a long moment. There was sincerity in her words, yet he remembered what Vail had said about her thespian skills. "What I really need, Deirdre, is not hack. What I really need is you."

Her frown vanished as he pulled her down on the bed and rolled atop her. With one hand he brushed the dark hair from her neck, then stroked her cheek gently.

"There is one problem," he said quietly. "I have not fed on a woman for many days. I may not be..."

She shushed him with a finger to his lips. "I am yours, Baris, in all ways."

Without another word, he bit into her neck.

He sucked ravenously at her blood, feeling it course like wildfire through his body, giving him a strength he had not felt for days. His body responded with equal power and intensity. He pressed against her, his heart pounding. He wanted her. By the Sovereign, how he wanted her! Yet, Vail's words hammered at the back of his mind, thoughts of Anika at his heart. Both kept him from fulfilling the desire. And he had to know the truth, had to know if Deirdre was really capable of all that Vail claimed. He needed proof. But how?

The answer came to him almost as quickly as the question. He tightened his grip, pulling her closer, feeding almost with a frenzy.

"Baris?" she protested, a note of fear in her husky voice. "Baris, slow down. Please."

He ignored her, tightening his grip even more. He heard her give a short gasp, then felt her push against him.

"Stop!" she ordered. "Stop! You're taking too much. You don't know what you're doing!"

But he did. He was going to force her to use magic. He was going to see for himself just how powerful she really was. Or he was going to kill her trying.

Sudden, severe pain tore through him, sending him rolling to one side with a gasp. Deirdre leapt from the bed, her hand at her still-bleeding neck. She glared at Baris as he sat up.

"Just what were you trying to do?" she demanded.

He sat still, trying to shake off the effects of the magic jolt she had delivered. Finally, he found his voice. "I thought you didn't have much magic, Deirdre."

"I...I don't," she stammered, going from rage to confusion so quickly it almost made him dizzy.

He rose, buoyed by the strength of her blood.

"I thought you couldn't focus on your magic when you were frightened." A wild look came into her eyes and Baris reached out to grip her by the wrist. He pulled her to him, his anger beginning to swell. "You didn't even ask me where I've been for the past week."

"I...I assumed you were lost, looking for Timmora. For me. After all, you're here."

"Because you brought me here," he pointed out.

"What? How could I bring you here? I didn't even know where you were!"

"And that man just happened to find me? Just happened to stumble upon me in that huge forest out there?"

"Yes! It was luck, Baris! I sent out more than one man. Someone was bound to find you."

"Stop!" he snapped. "I don't want to hear any more lies, Deirdre. You brought me here. You appeared to me, you guided me. It was your magic, Deirdre. Magic you claimed you didn't have. Just as it was your magic that made that man in the alley attack you, and that man at Quentin's house want to possess you. It was your magic that drove Anika away from me and then took me away from Anika."

She stared at him in astonishment, then tried to wrest away from him. He maintained his firm grip.

"No, Baris." She stopped fighting him and instead took a step closer, all innocent concern and sincerity. "You have it all wrong. I did nothing to Anika. Nothing to you. I swear."

He glared at her. "Do you swear by your god, Deirdre? Because if you do, you are damned."

"Baris, I don't know what you're talking about. Why are you so angry with me? What did I do to cause this?" Tears began to roll down her cheeks; her dark eyes were aswim with injured honor.

Baris swallowed hard, his emotions abruptly tumbling uncertainly.

"You lied to me," he accused plaintively, then felt his convictions returning as he remembered all that had happened, all that Vail had told him. "You kept me from the Lair, from my son, from finding Anika." He shoved her away so hard that she stumbled and fell to the floor by the bed. "Just what did you do with Anika anyway? Where did you send her?" Another thought abruptly crossed his mind. "And Thale? Did you cause that snake to attack him? Was that your doing as well? To get him out of the way?" He rubbed his face. "By the sovereign! Vail was right about everything!"

"Vail?" Deirdre spat.

"Yes, Vail. Who did you think was caring for me this past week? Who do you think helped me overcome my addiction? It was hell, Deirdre. Pure hell. And now--now it would seem that I will need to start over again. Why, Deirdre? Why did you do this to me?"

In that moment, she finally gave up the subterfuge. She drew a deep, slow breath, her lip curled in a savage sneer.

"I did not do anything to you, Baris," she snarled. "You did it to yourself. You were the one who enslaved Antyn, who used the hack even after he was dead. I tried to help you get off of it, Baris. Have you forgotten that?"

Baris frowned, rubbing at his temples as confusion returned. He could not clear his thoughts, could not seem to focus. "I haven't forgotten. But Vail said..."

"Vail!" She said the name as though it made her want to retch. "And you would believe him over me? He doesn't like me, Baris. He never has. He would like nothing more than to see me wedded to Holt, to become nothing more than a slave to another man. He would say anything to turn you against me."

"Why? Why should he?"

She threw up her hands. "Why? Because he's jealous. Jealous of my magic. And his lack of it. It's no small knowledge that he is inept. And even though I'm not considered gifted by any stretch of the imagination, he is not even close to my prowess. Why wouldn't he be jealous?"

Baris considered the words. True, he had not seen Vail display any great amount of magic at all. Perhaps it was as she said. He sagged onto the bed, his thoughts whirling in confusion. "This room reeks of magic. What were you doing?"

"I was trying to find Anika for you, Baris," Deirdre snapped. "Even after all that happened, the way you hurt me, I wanted to help you. And do you know what? I did find her. But she's with another Vector now. Apparently she has made her choice. Don't you see?" She approached him, dropped to her knees, gripped his hands in hers, kissed his palm. "She wasn't lying. She did indeed want you to leave. She doesn't want you, Baris. We can be together now. Like we were before. Don't you remember, Baris? Don't you remember how wonderful it was? I love you, Baris. I've loved you forever."

For a moment, his anger faltered. Memories crowded his mind, clutched his heart. Memories of holding her, caressing her, making passionate love to her. He ached to do so again.

Yet, Vail's voice hammered at his mind. He shook himself. "You love me?" he cried. "You destroyed me!"

"No, Baris, no. I showed you life as it really was. I showed you how it could be with a woman who loved you, cared for you, wanted you. Anika couldn't offer you that. She doesn't love you the way I do. She never has."

Baris looked into the dark depths of her eyes, suddenly just very tired.

"I love you, Baris," she said softly. "I would do anything for you. Anika doesn't deserve you."

Baris hesitated, then decided to play his last card. "Just as she didn't deserve Ris?"

She seemed startled by his question. "Ris? How did you..." She drew back, anger again twisting her face. "Vail, no doubt. I'll have to do something about his mouth. He talks too much."

Baris yanked his hands away, tore his gaze from hers, stood up and moved out of her reach. "No, Deirdre, you won't be hurting anyone again. Not Vail, not Anika, not me."

She opened her mouth to retort, but at that moment the door slammed open. Vail and Baul stumbled inside, Honey close behind. Deirdre turned on them in a rage.

Baris felt magic snap outward and he gasped. Vail grimaced but stood his ground. His gaze shifted to Baris.

"Are you all right?"

"Yes, I'm fine," he managed. "What are you doing here?"

"We thought you might need some help."

"You've helped quite enough, Vail!" Deirdre spat. "What lies have you been filling his head with?"

"Lies?" Vail laughed aloud. "No lies, Deirdre, and you know it."

"What I know is that you have once again interfered in my life. What is it with you and Anika, Vail? Do you get some perverse pleasure out of seeing me unhappy?"

"What is it with *you*, Deirdre? Do you get some perverse pleasure from another's pain?"

"I do nothing of the sort! I helped Baris! I was there when Anika wasn't. I am not the one who told him to leave. I am not the one who refused to let him touch me."

"I'll just bet you weren't," Baul muttered.

Rage darkened Deirdre's face. Her hands balled into fists at her sides and her eyes narrowed, then she suddenly smirked, her gazed shooting to Vail.

"Oh, by the gods! This isn't still about that stupid lamb is it?" Her mocking tone rang through the room.

Baris looked from one to the other, confusion gripping him. Vail turned scarlet, his own hands doubling into fists, though he was shaking. Deirdre threw back her head and laughed.

"Gods, Vail! It was a lamb! It was food!"

"It was a pet!" Vail nearly screamed. "It was a gift from my father. It was all I had left to remember him by. And you slaughtered it!"

"It was food!" Deirdre shrieked. "And it was delicious!"

Baris gasped out loud, not so much because of her words as from the tone of them. They were hard, cold and cruel, tormenting Vail even as tears gathered in his eyes. It may have been years gone past but it was clearly evident that Vail still carried a deep hurt from the incident.

Deirdre spun back to face Baris, her eyes wide, as if she had forgotten he stood there.

"It's not what you think, Baris," she cried. "He's making more of this than there was."

Everything Vail had said about Deirdre, about her calculating, manipulative ways, came flooding back to Baris. Watching her a moment ago as she berated Vail, he saw no compassion on her face, no warmth or love in her eyes. She had merely found a way to use words and past memories as a weapon. A very powerful weapon that left Vail trembling and glassy-eyed with renewed pain.

She must have guessed his thoughts, for she grasped his hand in hers. "Baris, don't! You can't believe him! He's just doing this to keep us apart! He would do anything to make me unhappy. I'll admit that I did a horrible thing. But I was a child. We had dozens of lambs, raised for meat. I simply chose the wrong one for dinner. I made a mistake."

"A mistake?" Vail cried, his voice catching. "It was no mistake, Deirdre and you know it. You stole Snowball right out of my..." He broke off, flushing, then startled when Honey gave him a gentle hug of understanding.

"You've lost, Deirdre," Vail said tightly. "Admit it and leave Baris alone."

"I think this is Baris' choice to make, Vail. Not yours. Why don't you be a good boy and run along?" Deirdre brushed one hand through the air.

"Not without Baris," Vail retorted. "In fact, I think some council elders will be very interested in the way you've been using your magic recently."

Deirdre whirled on him. "Don't you dare threaten me, Vail!" she snarled.

Baris felt magic explode outward, only it wasn't aimed at Vail. It went directly to Honey. The young woman's breath caught in her throat, her eyes went wide and she stumbled backward gasping, her smooth face contorted in agony.

"No!" Vail shrieked and brought his own magic forward. "Leave her alone!"

"Enough!" Baris snapped. He threw his Vector magic over Deirdre, trapping her in her own evil. Her magic rebounded and she shrieked with pain.

Honey collapsed into Vail's arms, trying to catch her breath even as Baris advanced on Deirdre.

"It is obvious you are not who I thought you were, Deirdre," he seethed. "Vail and Anika were right. You are far too powerful to remain with humans. And apparently you are too strong to be controlled by the priests or Holt. Still, I cannot allow you to continue to manipulate others, to hurt them, to tear their lives apart."

"What are you going to do?" Vail asked quietly.

"I don't know," Baris admitted, rubbing at his face with one hand.

"I do," Baul put in quietly. "I know someone who can control her and her magic."

Deirdre gasped, opening her mouth to protest, but the Vector Sovereign arrived in the room seconds later, as if he had been waiting for the call. Baris stared in outright shock. It was obvious Baul had seen what he could not. There was indeed a place for Deirdre, a place that would keep her from hurting anyone else.

Baris watched at the Sovereign approached Deirdre. He could see the desire in Darius' eyes as he appraised Deirdre thoughtfully, then extended his hand to her. She backed away. Baris felt her reach for her magic, then watched as her face paled when she found she could not. Her gaze shot to Baris, pleading in the dark depths.

"No. Don't let him take me, Baris. Please. We can go away together. Anika has Thale and--and another Vector to care for her. What do I have?"

Darius smiled. "You now have me."

Deirdre reluctantly shifted her gaze to meet the Sovereign's. Again, Baris felt her attempt to repel his hypnotic magic but he was far too strong for her. Trembling, she accepted his hand, though tears stood in her eyes. Darius drew her close.

Despite what she had done, it broke Baris' heart to see her like this, looking like a lost child being punished. Still, he knew it had to be. She had eyes only for the Sovereign now. He had completely enchanted her and, with a wave of his hand, they both disappeared.

Chapter Twenty-One

"I can't do this," Baris said, turning away.

Vail turned him back around. "Yes, you can. Anika's been waiting for you."

"But, Vail, how can I face her?"

"She knows everything, Baris," Baul said.

"Then there's nothing left to say," Baris mumbled, though he knew in his heart that wasn't true. He looked up as another Vector strode toward him. Quentin. Baris had thought it very strange that Quentin had turned out to be the Vector harboring Anika, caring for her, helping her recover. The fact was, she had shown up at his house in pursuit of Deirdre and Baris. The thought that Anika had been following him, searching for him, warmed Baris' heart. At the same time, it sent more guilt and despair raging through him. He recalled days when he hadn't even thought of her at all.

Quentin had listened to her story, remembering Baris and Deirdre well. But when he told Anika that he had sent them away, she had collapsed, finally overcome by her fatigue and grief. Quentin had taken her in, had contacted Darius and then had gently nurtured Anika back to health. To Baris' vast relief, Quentin had not even tried to seduce Anika. He had fed on her only to help her, with no other ramifications. Baris wished he had the same control over his own body. He found himself viewing Quentin with gratitude and respect. And embarrassment. He could not forget his first meeting with the Vector Elder, the scene he had caused. Even being here in Quentin's home was trying, and Baris wished he could simply escape. But there would be no escape. He had to face both Quentin and Anika.

"You haven't gone in yet?" Quentin asked now, a smile quirking his lips.

"I...I can't, Elder," Baris stammered.

"Nonsense." Quentin took his arm, opened the door and fairly shoved him into the bedchamber.

Baris gasped as Anika rose from a long armless couch near the fireplace. Her pale-blue silk gown swirled around her ankles, hugging her form. Her hair hung in soft, dark curls past her shoulders and her blue eyes were fixed on his. Gone were the dark circles of illness, the pale complexion. She was vibrant and healthy, her cheeks made rosy by both the fire and the blush that crept over them as she viewed Baris.

Baris couldn't take his eyes from her and actually stumbled when Quentin gave him another gentle shove before retreating and closing the door.

For a long moment neither of them spoke, then Anika extended her hand. Baris sobbed and covered his face with both hands.

"Ani, I'm so sorry," he wept. "I'm so sorry."

He heard her approach, stiffened as her warm hands touched his, pulling them away from his face. He stared into the blue depths of her eyes, seeing no condemnation, only love. With another sob, he gathered her into his arms, murmuring his apologies over and over. She held to him as tightly as he did to her. Long moments passed before Baris regained his composure.

"Where were you, Ani?" he asked, pulling back. "I looked and looked for you. Where did you go?"

She sighed, and pulled him toward the couch. They sank down together, Baris holding to her hands in desperation. After a moment, she spoke. "I want to apologize, Baris," she said softly. "For all of those horrible things I said to you, for the way I acted."

"You?" Baris cried. "You are not the one who needs to apologize, Ani. I am. While I cannot ask you to forget, or to even accept me again, I would ask that you forgive me."

She stroked his hair from his forehead. "Forgive you? Yes. Not accept you? I love you, Baris. You're the other part of my soul. I couldn't live without you." She wiped the tears from his cheeks, then kissed his hand. "We were both spelled. We have nothing to be guilty over. Nothing."

Baris winced, trying to divert the conversation. "Where did you go, Ani? I searched for you, but I couldn't find you. Where did you go?"

"Away, Baris. Just away. I had no choice. Deirdre was too strong for me. She controlled me too completely. I couldn't resist her. At least, not until much later. The further I got from her, the more she was involved in working her spells on you, the weaker her hold over me became. I was finally able to throw off her spells but it took me many more days to regain enough of my health to travel. Then, I followed you." She gave him a small smile. "Did you really think I would give up on you so easily?"

He was silent a moment, his heart heavy with despair. He had no answer for that. And the question only served to further his own guilt over everything that had happened. All the while his beautiful wife was fighting for her own life, and his, he was enjoying himself with fancy clothing, food, entertainment, and Deirdre. He looked away, unable to meet her gaze.

Anika sighed. "I know all about Deirdre, Baris. Everything. The Spells, the stories...everything. Including--" She paused, as if unsure how to continue. Finally, she tipped her chin up, took a deep breath and said, "Including the fact that she now carries your child."

Baris sucked in his breath in horror. He had not known, had no idea, had not even considered the possibility.

"No," he breathed. "No, she...no!" He pulled away, embarrassment and agonizing remorse flooding through him. He buried his face in his hands, his heart twisting in agony, his words clouded by his tears. "Forgive me, Ani, please forgive me."

"Baris," she whispered. She again pulled his hands away from his face. "I do not condemn you for this. You forget. I know Deirdre. I know what she is capable of."

"But this..." He shook his head. "I have betrayed you, our vows. Oh, Anika, for so long I never knew what it meant to love someone, to really love them. But over the past few weeks, I have learned so much. I love you and Thale with all of my heart. I cannot see my life without either of you."

"And I cannot see my life without you," Anika told him. "I love you just as deeply, Baris."

He stared into her eyes, tears blurring his vision. "How can you, Ani?" he whispered. "I'm a failure, in every way." He sagged at the mere word. He hadn't told her about the hack, had made Vail promise not to as well. He didn't want her to know. It was something he wanted to conquer on his own. Perhaps then he would feel in control again. He knew it was going to take a long time to regain his self-esteem, his pride, his acceptance of himself.

"Baris, the only way you will fail me is if you let Deirdre win at this. Her only goal was to separate us. Will you let her win?"

"No," he murmured, although he wondered if she already had. Could it ever be the same between him and Anika? How would she be able to forget his unfaithfulness? Especially with Deirdre carrying his child? The thought was almost too much to bear.

"Deirdre's child--" he started, unsure exactly what he wanted to say, to do.

Anika stopped him. "Darius told me it would be raised in the Lair."

"In the Lair?" Baris couldn't seem to get his emotions to settle. He felt both a great relief at that news and a great sadness.

"Papa?"

Baris whirled as Thale toddled into the room. Vail winked at Baris and pulled the door closed. Baris fell to one knee and took Thale into his arms. "Thale! My boy!" He kissed the child gently, repeatedly, until Thale pushed away. Baris stared at him, his heart swelling with love. "Are you feeling better?" he asked, his voice cracking on the words, emotion threatening to close up his throat.

Thale nodded, then stuck his finger out. "Bite gone."

Baris stared at the chubby little finger, tears blurring his vision. "Bite gone," he repeated, and kissed Thale's finger, then once again drew the boy into his arms. He sat down on the couch, holding Thale on his lap.

The little boy put one chubby arm around Baris' neck, the other around Anika's, and drew his parents together in a tight hug. "All better now," he announced.

Baris looked into his wife's eyes, saw only love and passion in the blue depths and his heart again melted for this woman, his lifemate.

"All better now," she whispered.

Baris smiled, and brought his lips to hers in a gentle kiss speaking of forgiveness, acceptance and love from the heart.

You can find ALL our books up on our website at:

http://www.writers-exchange.com

all our fantasy novels:

http://www.writers-exchange.com/category/genres/fantasy/

JennaKay Francis has been writing since she was 12 years old. She has written in many different genres - science fiction, childrens, mainstream, poetry - but truly found her voice and love in fantasy. She writes fantasy adventure, fantasy romance, dark fantasy and children's picture books.

Her first official publication was a children's poem that was the Grand Prize winner in a contest sponsored by Half-Price Books. Her prize was a $500.00 gift certificate at Half Price Books: something she took great delight in spending. She has been published in several local newsletters, several print magazines, as well as numerous online magazines in both fiction and non-fiction.

Jenna lives in the beautiful Pacific Northwest with her husband, their three delightful children, two wild cats, a chihuahua that thinks he's really a dog, one rat, one anole and a several tanks of tropical fish, frogs and newts.

Oh, yeah, and a forest full of elves, fairies and magic.

JennaKay was also Writers Exchange's Senior editor for many years.

You can keep track of all her books on her author page:

http://www.writers-exchange.com/Jennakay-Francis/

If you want to read more about other books by this author, they are listed on the following pages...

Blood Bred Series

{Fantasy: Vampire}

Book 1: Gift of Blood

Jaeger needs blood. Half Vector, half human, newly coming of age, Jaeger is now drawn to human blood for the first time in his already long life.

Rhiannon, a witch, has too much iron in her blood to safely live. She wants to propose a partnership with the Vectors, but, before she can approach them, she's attacked and left for dead beneath a pier. Jaeger finds her unconscious and bleeding. Fighting against the lure of her blood, he takes her to a place of safety instead. His actions set them both on a course of pain, hunger, terror and love. Can he save her from himself?
Publisher: http://www.writers-exchange.com/Gift-Of-Blood/

Book 2: From the Heart

Baris has everything: A wife he worships, a child he adores, a life of comfort and security. But his idyllic existence changes suddenly and dramatically, with no explanation. Anika, his wife, shuns him and orders him to leave her side. His child claims his mother is not really his mama. And Dierdre, a devastatingly beautiful young woman slides into Baris' life with seduction on her mind.

When Baris attempts to help his wife, she flees, leaving him alone with their son and Dierdre. To add to his agony, the child is bitten by a poisonous snake and Baris has no choice but to take him to the Lair to save his life. Once reunited with Dierdre, the pair set off in search of Anika. But, as the days turn to weeks with no sign of his wife, Baris must accept the possibility that she has no wish to be found.

As his life grows increasingly entangled with Dierdre's, he makes the mistake of feeding on a young man addicted to a powerful drug called Hack. Baris is soon addicted as well and must struggle to reclaim everything that he once held dear...or die.

Publisher: http://www.writers-exchange.com/From-the-Heart/

Book 3: New Beginnings

A powerful Vector roams the dark alleys and streets searching for his next victim. But he he's not interested in those with normal blood--only those whose veins runs blood thick with the highly-addictive drug Hack. If Adan can't find someone who's just ingested the potent drug, he has no compunction about using his powers to coerce them to do so before he feeds.

For Vector Sovereign Darius, Adan has become a problem he needs to fix...

Publisher: http://www.writers-exchange.com/New-Beginnings/

Free Spirit

{Fantasy Romance}

Diesa de Tyronmen escapes from a brutal master only to be sold to an elf. Though mesmerized by his beauty, Diesa struggles for her freedom...and against her own growing love for her new master. Was she purchased only to win a wager? And, as her mother had claimed, will an elf claim her heart with his words, her very soul with his touch?

Publisher: http://www.writers-exchange.com/Free-Spirit/

The Faery Sickness

{Fantasy Romance}

Vala Kalei was saved from death by the fae but condemned by her own neighbors. When she goes to the faery realm and retrieves the babies that have been dying, she opens up another world filled with mystery, pain, heartache...and love.

Publisher: http://www.writers-exchange.com/The-Faery-Sickness/

Guardians of Glede Universe:

Beginnings Series

{Fantasy: Young Adult}

When the balance of power is threatened in the land of Glede, the powerful Triskelion calls for its master.

Book 1: The Triskelion

The Triskelion, a powerful magical amulet, once torn into two parts to protect the world of Glede, now must be found and re-united to save Glede. Two boys are summoned by the magic of the Triskelion to perform this dangerous task -Treyas Beckering, a 14 year old elf from Bailiwycke in the west; and 13 year old Jannson van Tannen, the newly orphaned King of Odora Dava to the east. Both will endure more than they ever thought possible, and both will become men in the process.

Publisher: http://www.writers-exchange.com/The-Triskelion/

Book 2: Dark Prince

Prince Rugan Merripen, once thought to be the rightful master of the Triskelion's magic, was cast aside by the medallion itself when it chose his half-brother Treyas Beckering as master. Now Rugan is on a quest to regain the magic and power he thinks is rightfully his. Befriended and manipulated by Vaalde, an evil sorcerer who has only his own goals in mind, Rugan attempts to drain Glede of elfin magic. Once gone, only sorcery magic will remain and Vaalde can then rule the world. It is up to King Jansson and Treyas to stop him and restore the balance of magic once again. Each boy will face what seem to be insurmountable odds, and both will discover that friends are there to depend on in times of travail. And Treyas will move towards a destiny that he never envisioned.

Publisher: http://www.writers-exchange.com/Dark-Prince/

Book 3: Sorcerer's Pool

Firmly embedded into Prince Rugan's mind, the sorcerer Vaalde once more manipulates Prince Rugan into wresting the Triskelion magic from Treyas Beckering Merripen, now the Crown Prince of Lidgerwood. This time Vaalde spirits King Jansson van Tannen and Treyas to Karsaba, a land void of magic and the ability to drain memory. Three days outside of magic and their memories will be wiped clean. Unfortunately for Vaalde, King Kyel Sylvain has hitched a ride. The black elf, reknowned for his magical prowess will prove to be a formidable adversary. But will Jansson and Treyas survive the strange power of Karsaba or will they lose everything that makes them who they are?

Publisher: http://www.writers-exchange.com/Sorcerers-Pool/

Book 4: Dragons of Mere Odain

Far away in the land of Mere Odain, a dragon calls out for help to her master--Pepin Merripen, now living as the son of Crown Prince Treyas Merripen and his wife, Cynthe. Pepin must answer, or die. Shocked and terrified, Treyas gathers his closest friends, and goes to Mere Odain. But the country is in turmoil. An ethnic cleansing is going on--any black or brown skinned person must die. Treyas is determined to save his young son's life even if it means taking on the whole of the Keltin Empire and ending a war 40 years in the making.

Publisher: http://www.writers-exchange.com/Dragons-of-Mere-Odain/

Book 5: Dragon Master

Pepin Merripen learns that the two countries that had promised to protect the dragons, his dragons, have withdrawn their forces. Furious at this betrayal, he goes to Karsaba to take council with Mere Odain's young Queen. Although his father is willing to let Pepin resolve this situation, he soon finds out that Pepin has disappeared. Treyas follows his son's trail, but it ends where magic begins.

Increasingly worried, Treyas attempts to follow the magical trail and ends up in Northern Karsaba. It soon becomes apparent that he has more to deal with than a disgruntled runaway youth. A powerful magiker claiming to be Pepin's birth mother has summoned him, and she will stop at nothing to see his control over the dragons become her own. With Pepin at her command, and thereby his dragons, she intends to rule not only Karsaba, but any land she chooses. It is up to Treyas and his friends to make sure that doesn't happen. But will Treyas lose his son to the powerful pull of the dragons?

Publisher: http://www.writers-exchange.com/Dragonmaster/

Book 6: For the Love of Dragons

Pepin Merripen, now a young man of fourteen, has forged a strong bond with the elves. So when Queen El'leigh of Mere Odain informs him that the dragons have disappeared, he is torn between his allegiance and his love for the dragons. Still, he is steadfast in his loyalty to his father, Treyas Merripen, and refuses El'leigh's request to join her in the search.

Furious, El'leigh sends Pepin's love, Nila, to the wilds of South Kelta, the last known place of the dragons. As she suspected, Pepin quickly follows before any harm befalls Nila. No sooner have the two young lovers arrived in Kelta, than they are captured by Keltin warriors, who quickly ascertain that they have the DragonMaster in their grasp. And if they can force Pepin to make the dragons do their bidding, they'll regain their lost advantage in Mere Odain. All they have to do is use Nila as incentive.

Publisher: http://www.writers-exchange.com/For-The-Love-Of-Dragons/

Guardians of Glede Universe Continued:

Next Generation Series

{Fantasy: Young Adult}

Return to the land of Glede for new adventures with the next generation!

Book 1: Caves of Challenge

Their heads filled with stories of adventures spun by their father and uncles, Princes Vantann and Thomlin Merripen decide to have an adventure of their own. Through an old book, they learn of the Caves of Challenge. If they can survive the challenges within the caves, they will emerge as men.

Blackmailed by their young friend, Shuri, the boys agree to take her along. Before they trio has a chance to adequately prepare, however, they are sent to the Caves by haphazard magic. Once there, Shuri and Vantann are captured by War Gnomes, while Thomlin is lost in a dark swamp. His only consolation is that, somehow, he has snagged King Jansson van Tannen on the magic strand.

Jansson is reassuring, telling Thomlin that there will be a rescue party sent out and all they need do is wait. But the rescue party is having trouble of their own, and they find much more than they bargained for in the Caves. The question now becomes, who will be forced to stay in the Caves of Challenge forever.

Publisher: http://www.writers-exchange.com/Caves-of-Challenge/

Book 2: Blood Sacrifice

Tormented with guilt over the happenings in the Caves of Challenge, Prince Vantann Merripen watches over his siblings with a critical, judgmental and sometimes violent scrutiny. Prince Thomlin finally rebels and accidentally sets the course for an even more dangerous adventure than the one he and his brother endured in the Caves. Swept into a land that demonizes the second-born of twins, forbids magic, and is currently being terrorized by a coven of Nydiri, the twins very survival is threatened.

Any use of magic carries the penalty of death. Contact with the coven means the same, for the Nydiri are actively seeking twins to complete a powerful spell they intend to weave at the height of a mysterious orange moon. And elvin twins are especially prized.

Publisher: http://www.writers-exchange.com/Blood-Sacrifice/

Book 3: The Coven

Pepin reclaims his title as DragonMaster, not fully understanding the ramifications of such a move. Is his allegiance with the elves, or with Mere Odain? The announcement of his decision couldn't have come at a worse time – the Crown Prince is to leave the next day on a diplomatic visit to Dalziel.

Once in Dalziel, things rapidly begin to fall apart. Politically, Kyel and Jansson are at each other's throats, Vantann and Thomlin make friends in the wrong places, and Treyas finds out that his SoulMate and squire, Druce Sinclair, suffers from a horribly painful and incurable disease.

To top it off, Treyas discovers that Dalziel has been overrun with Nydiri with the power of Illusion in their grasp.

When Vantann, Thomlin and others disappear, Treyas must find a way to free the captives and destroy the Nydiri threat once and for all...

Publisher: http://www.writers-exchange.com/The-Coven/

Book 4: Fire Stone

Stranded after a river float trip goes horribly wrong, Brann van Tannen and his friends Tavin, Elek and Janna are caught by slave traders. To make matters worse, on board the barge are three trolls, descendants of the tribe that destroyed Mayfaire and killed Brann's grandfather. Brann will need to rely on all of the strength, wisdom and courage his father instilled in him while their lives are changed beyond wildest imagination.

Publisher: http://www.writers-exchange.com/Fire-Stone/

Book 5: The Fane Queen

Attempting to escape the past can have devastating consequences...

Ask Tavin Sylvain, who is trying to forget all about the abuse he suffered at the hands of the trolls six months earlier.

Ask Kitiara, who would like to escape her sordid past in Kartonn, where she was known as the Princess of Pleasure.

Or ask King Jansson van Tannen, who would like nothing better than to keep his family intact and not have to face the possibility of losing one of his own beloved children to fate.

When the past rears its ugly head, all three are thrown into turmoil. Tavin, Brann and Kitiara are lost in Karsaba, without magic, without direction, without hope. And in the middle of a troll invasion. In a race against time, King Jansson and King Kyel gather their closest friends and allies to find the children before the trolls find them first.

Publisher: http://www.writers-exchange.com/The-Fane-Queen/

Book 6: Battle for Argathia

A desperate plea for help, written on a scroll and sent with magic, falls into the wrong hands, and with a few misplace words, Treyas' young daughter activates the spell, sending her and her friends to a world controlled by the Albino.

The Albino, not content with being dictator of only one world, now has a hostage--and one of royal pedigree--with which to extend his empire. It is up to Treyas and his companions to stop the Albino and free the world he has claimed as his own.

Publisher: http://www.writers-exchange.com/Battle-for-Argathia/

Guardians of Glede Universe Continued:

Reckonings Series

{Fantasy: Young Adult}

Return to the land of Glede during a time when the Nydiri intend to destroy not only Treyas but the whole of the elven empire.

Book 1: Dukker's Revenge

Elek is missing and Dukker has returned. The Nydiri will not stop until not only Treyas is destroyed but the whole of the elven empire. When the palace is infiltrated, chaos ensues. Floy, the son of a visiting dignitary, becomes an unwitting pawn in Dukker's plans. Through him, Dukker captures three of the royal youth.

Treyas and his companions set out to rescue the young people, but their TravelSpell is severely compromised, sending them in different directions. They will all need to rely on new friends, and a powerful, mysterious dagger, to set things right and defeat the Nydiri.

Publisher: http://www.writers-exchange.com/Rukkers-Revenge/

Nitesh

{Fantasy Romance}

Thalassa, a sea-witch, is captured when the warlord Rhaeven sends his troops to her small village. After the hard life she's already lived, she's resigned to her fate. Married at a young age to an abusive man she doesn't love, she's secretly glad to see her husband die. Now, pregnant, enslaved and stricken with a deadly disease, she only waits for her own death to release her from the torment that is life.

Elfin Crown Prince of Diraenia, Terran, must choose a mate and produce an heir before his thirtieth birthday or risk forfeiting the crown to his youngest brother Unwin. Time is running out. Terran is twenty-nine, his fiancee is dead, and he believes Unwin responsible despite the lack of proof. To make matters worse, Terran's other brother Sinclair has disappeared, and Terran fears the worst.

Bothered by a strange, haunting beat of drums no one can hear but Terran, the Crown Prince thoughts continually turn to a brief encounter he shared with a young woman from Zal. For three days, he'd walked her back to her village, delivering her to her pre-ordained life there. For three days, he fell in love with the wife of a woman who could never be his. When he returned to his own palace, he'd seen the emptiness and despair of his own life.

The drums call to Terran until he can longer deny his own need to revisit the village where he'd fallen in love. If he sees Thalassa one last time, can he make himself let go?

Publisher: http://www.writers-exchange.com/Nitesh/

If you want to read more about other Fantasy novels by this publisher, they are listed on...

http://www.writers-exchange.com/category/genres/fantasy/

You can find ALL our books up on our website at:

http://www.writers-exchange.com